HAWKSONG

HAWKSONG

Amelia Atwater-Rhodes

LAUREL-LEAF BOOKS

Published by
Dell Laurel-Leaf
an imprint of
Random House Children's Books
a division of Random House, Inc.
New York

Visit us on the Web! www.randomhouse.com/teens

Educators and librarians, for a variety of teaching tools, visit us at
www.randomhouse.com/teachers

ISBN: 0-440-23803-X

RL: 6.0

Reprinted by arrangement with Delacorte Press

Printed in the United States of America

September 2004

10 9 8 7 6 5 4 3 2 1

OPM

Hawksong
is dedicated to my mother, Susan Atwater-Rhodes,
for everything she has given me and everything I am now.

she
o'saerre'Kain'hena
Mehay'hena-ke-namra'la'Susan Atwater-Rhodes
ke-leonMehay-ke'ke-la'maen'leonShe'hena

Also,
I give thanks to:
My friend and fellow writer, Kyle Bladow,
for his faith in me.
Ginna Kruger, for all her help and interest.
Kelly Henry, for her friendship.

ke'ke
la-varl'teska-a
eh'ha'la'Kyle Bladow-ke-wim-maen'la'fide
Ginna Kruger-ke-ravilla'falmay
Kelly Henry-ke-ha'Anhamirak

Thanks from all my heart and soul.
o'la'lo'Mehay'teska

a'le-Ahnleh

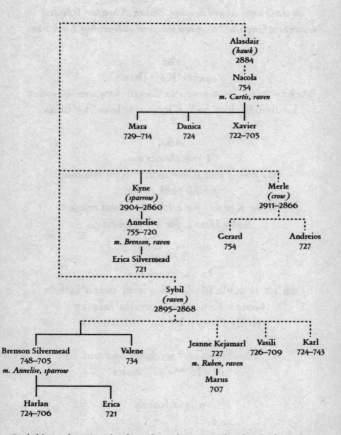

Alasdair
(hawk)
2884

Nacola
754
m. Curtis, raven

Mara
729–714

Danica
724

Xavier
722–705

Kyne
(sparrow)
2904–2860

Annelise
755–720
m. Brenson, raven

Erica Silvermead
721

Merle
(crow)
2911–2866

Gerard
754

Andreios
727

Sybil
(raven)
2895–2868

Brenson Silvermead
748–705
m. Annelise, sparrow

Valene
734

Jeanne Kejamarl
727
m. Ruben, raven

Marus
707

Vasili
726–709

Karl
724–743

Harlan
724–706

Erica
721

Dashed lines indicate not only a lapse of several generations, but also an indirect relation.

HIFTERS

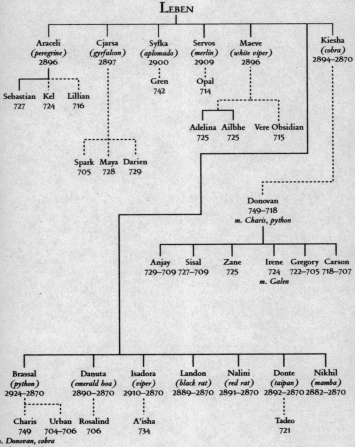

LEBEN

Araceli (*peregrine*) 2896
Cjarsa (*gyrfalcon*) 2897
Syfka (*aplomado*) 2900
Servos (*merlin*) 2909
Maeve (*white viper*) 2896
Kiesha (*cobra*) 2894–2870

Sebastian 727
Kel 724
Lillian 716

Gren 742

Opal 714

Adelina 725
Ailbhe 725
Vere Obsidian 715

Spark 705
Maya 728
Darien 729

Donovan 749–718
m. *Charis, python*

Anjay 729–709
Sisal 727–709
Zane 725
Irene 724 m. *Galen*
Gregory 722–705
Carson 718–707

Brassal (*python*) 2924–2870
Danuta (*emerald boa*) 2890–2870
Isadora (*viper*) 2910–2870
Landon (*black rat*) 2889–2870
Nalini (*red rat*) 2891–2870
Donte (*taipan*) 2892–2870
Nikhil (*mamba*) 2882–2870

Charis 749
Urban 704–706
Rosalind 706

A'isha 734

Tadeo 721

m. *Donovan, cobra*
(see cobras)

PROLOGUE

They say the first of my kind was a woman named Alasdair, a human raised by hawks. She learned the language of the birds and was gifted with their form.

It is a pretty myth, I admit, but few actually believe it. No record remains of her life.

No record except for the feathers in every avian's hair, even when otherwise we appear human, and the wings I can grow when I choose—and of course the beautiful golden hawk's form that is as natural to me as the legs and arms I wear normally.

This myth is one of the stories we hear as children, but it says nothing of reality or the hard lessons we are taught later.

Almost before a child of my kind learns to fly, she learns to hate. She learns of war. She learns of the race that calls itself the serpiente. She learns that they are

1

untrustworthy, that they are liars and loyal to no one. She learns to fear the garnet eyes of their royal family even though she will probably never see them.

What she never learns is how the fighting began. No, that has been forgotten. Instead she learns that they murdered her family and her loved ones. She learns that these enemies are evil, that their ways are not hers and that they would kill her if they could.

That is all she learns.

This is all I have learned.

Days and weeks and years, and all I know is bloodshed. I hum the songs my mother once sang to me and wish for the peace they promise. It's a peace my mother has never known, nor her mother before her.

How many generations? How many of our soldiers fallen?

And why?

Meaningless hatred: the hatred of an enemy without a face. No one knows why we fight; they only know that we will continue until we win a war it is too late to win, until we have avenged too many dead to avenge, until no one can remember peace anymore, even in songs.

Days and weeks and years.

My brother never returned last night.

Days and weeks and years.

How long until their assassins find me?

Danica Shardae
Heir to the Tuuli Thea

CHAPTER 1

I TOOK A DEEP BREATH TO STEADY MY NERVES and narrowly avoided retching from the sharp, well-known stench that surrounded me.

The smell of hot avian blood spattered on the stones, and cool serpiente blood that seemed ready to dissolve the skin off my hands if I touched it. The smell of burned hair and feathers and skin of the dead smoldered in the fire of a dropped lantern. Only the fall of rain all the night before had kept that fire from spreading through the clearing to the woods.

From the forest to my left, I heard the desperate, strangled cry of a man in pain.

I started to move toward the sound, but when I took a step through the trees in his direction, I came upon a sight that made my knees buckle, my breath freezing as I fell to the familiar body.

Golden hair, so like my own, was swept across the boy's eyes, closed forever now but so clear in my mind. His skin was gray in the morning light, covered with a light spray of dew. My younger brother, my only brother, was dead.

Like our sister and our father years ago, like our aunts and uncles and too many friends, Xavier Shardae was forever grounded. I stared at his still form, willing him to take a breath and open eyes whose color would mirror my own. I willed myself to wake up from this nightmare.

I could not be the last. The last child of Nacola Shardae, who was all the family I had left now.

I wanted to scream and weep, but a hawk does not cry, especially here on the battlefield, in the midst of the dead and surrounded only by her guards. She does not scream or beat the ground and curse the sky.

Among my kind, tears were considered a disgrace to the dead and shame among the living.

Avian reserve. It kept the heart from breaking with each new death. It kept the warriors fighting a war no one could win. It kept me standing when I had nothing to stand for but bloodshed.

I could not cry for my brother, though I wanted to.

I pushed the sounds away, forcing my lips not

to tremble. Only one heavy breath escaped me, wanting to be a sigh. I lifted my dry eyes to the guards who stood about me protectively in the woods.

"Take him home," I ordered, my voice wavering a bit despite my resolve.

"Shardae, you should come home, too."

I turned to Andreios, the captain of the most elite flight in the avian army, and took in the worried expression in his soft brown eyes. The crow had been my friend for years before he had been my guard, and I began to nod assent to his words.

Another cry from the woods made me freeze. I started toward it, but Andreios caught my arm just above the elbow. "Not that one, milady."

Normally I would have trusted his judgment without question, but not here on the battlefield. I had been walking these bloody fields whenever I could ever since I was twelve; I could not avert my eyes when we were in the middle of this chaos and someone was pleading, with what was probably his last breath, for help. "And why not, Andreios?"

The crow knew he was in trouble the instant I addressed him by his full name instead of his childhood nickname of Rei, but he kept on my heels as I stepped around the slain bodies and closer to the voice. The rest of his flight fell back, out of sight in their second forms—crows and ravens, mostly. They would take my brother home only when it did not mean leaving me alone here.

"Dani." In return, I knew Rei was serious when he lapsed into the informal and used *my* nickname, Dani, instead of a respectful title or my surname, Shardae. Even when we were alone, Rei rarely called me Danica. It was an entreaty to our lifelong friendship when he used that nickname where someone else could hear it, and so I paused to listen. "That's Gregory Cobriana. You don't want his blood on your hands."

For a moment the name meant nothing to me. With his hair streaked with blood and his expression a mask of pain, Gregory Cobriana could have been anyone's brother, husband or son. But then I recognized the stark black hair against his fair skin, the onyx signet ring on his left hand and, as he looked up, the deep garnet eyes that were a trademark of the Cobriana line, just as molten gold eyes were characteristic of my own family.

I did not have the energy to rage. Every emotion I had was cloaked in the shield of reserve I had learned since I was a chick.

Evidently the serpiente prince recognized me as well, for his pleas caught in his throat, and his eyes closed.

I stepped toward him and heard a flutter of movement as my guards moved closer, ready to intervene if the fallen man was a threat.

With all his various scratches and minor injuries, it was hard to tell where the worst of the damage was. I saw a broken leg, possibly a broken arm; either of those he could heal from.

What would I do if that was the worst? If he was hurt, but not too hurt to survive? This was the man who had led the soldiers that had killed my brother and his guards. Would I turn my back so the Royal Flight could finish what all these fallen fighters had not?

For a moment I thought of taking my knife and putting it in his heart or slitting his throat myself and ending the life this creature still held while my brother lay dead.

Despite my guards' protest, I went again to my knees, this time beside the enemy. I looked at that pale face and tried to summon the fury I needed.

His eyes fluttered open and met mine. A muddy shade of red, Gregory Cobriana's eyes were filled with pain, sorrow and fear. The fear struck me the most. This *boy* looked a couple of years younger than I was, too young to deserve this horror, too young to die.

Bile rose in my throat. I loved my brother, but I could not murder his killer. I could not look into the eyes of a boy terrified of death and shaking from pain and feel hatred. This was a life: serpiente, yes, but still a *life*; who was I to steal it?

Only as I recoiled did I see the wound on his stomach, where a knife had dragged itself raggedly across the soft flesh, one of the most painful of mortal blows. The attacker must have been killed before he could finish the deed.

Perhaps my brother had held the knife. Had he lain dying alone like this afterward?

I felt a sob choke my throat and couldn't stop it. Gregory Cobriana was the enemy, but here on the battlefield he was just another brother to another sister, fallen on the field. I could not cry for my own brother; he would not want me to. But I found myself crying for this hated stranger and the endless slaughter that I had almost contributed to.

I spun on Rei. "This is why this stupid war goes on. Because even when he's dying, you can only feel your hate," I spat, too quietly for the serpiente prince to hear me.

"If I was in this man's place, I would pray for someone to kneel by my side," I continued. "And I wouldn't care if that person was Zane Cobriana himself."

Rei knelt awkwardly beside me. For a moment, his hand touched my hand, unexpectedly. His gaze met mine, and I heard him sigh quietly with understanding.

I turned back to the serpiente. "I'm here; don't fret," I said as I smoothed black hair from Gregory's face.

His eyes filled with tears and he muttered something that sounded like "Thank you." Then he looked straight up at me and said, "End it. Please."

These words made me wince. I had been thinking the same thing just moments before, but even though I knew he was asking me to stop the pain, I did not want mine to be the hand that ended another's life.

"Dani?" Rei asked worriedly when a tear fell from my eyes onto Gregory's hand.

I shook my head and wrapped my hand around Gregory's cool one. The muscles tightened, and then he was gripping my hand like it was his last anchor to earth.

When I drew the knife from my waist, Rei caught my wrist and shook his head.

Quietly, so Gregory could not hear, I argued, "It could take him hours to die like this."

"Let the hours pass," Rei answered, though I could see the muscles in his jaw tighten. "Serpiente believe in mercy killing, but not when it's the other side who does it. Not when it's the heir to the Tuuli Thea who ends the life of one of their two surviving princes."

We sat in the field most of the day, until Gregory's grip on my hand loosened and his ragged breathing froze.

As I had often done for dying avian soldiers, I sang to pass the time, and to distract him from the pain. The songs were about freedom. They were about children, able to play and sing and dance without worrying that they would be harmed.

The song I loved most of all, though, was the one my mother used to sing to me when I was a child, before I had been given round-the-clock nurses, maids, servants and guards. It was from long before my mother had become a distant queen with too much dignity to show affection even to her last remaining daughter. I would have given up all the pampering and all the respect I had earned those past few years if I could have climbed into her arms and gone back to a time when I was still too young to understand that my father, my sister and now my brother had been butchered in this war, which had been going on so long nobody could tell anymore what it was about or who had started it.

I had heard of avians and serpiente who had lived five hundred years or more, but no one did that now. Not in a time when both sides slaughtered each other so frequently, and so efficiently.

The only male child left to inherit the serpiente throne was Zane Cobriana, a creature whose name was rarely mentioned in polite avian society, and if he died . . . hopefully the murderous royal house of the serpiente would die with him. Yet now that Gregory Cobriana, the youngest and last brother of our greatest enemy, was dead in front of me, I could not be grateful for the loss. All I could do was sing gently the old childhood lullaby called "Hawksong" that my mother had sung to me long ago.

> *I wish to you sunshine, my dear one,*
> *my dear one. And treetops for you to soar*
> *past. I wish to you innocence, my child, my*
> *child. I pray you don't grow up too fast.*
> *Never know pain, my dear one, my*
> *dear one. Nor hunger nor fear nor sorrow.*
> *Never know war, my child, my child.*
> *Remember your hope for tomorrow.*

BY THE TIME I found sleep that night, back in the Hawk's Keep, my throat was tight with too many tears unshed, screams unuttered and prayers whose words I could never seem to find.

CHAPTER 2

MY MOTHER, LADY NACOLA SHARDAE, WAS like a bronze statue as she watched the pyre consume yet another of her children on Mourner's Rock. Firelight gave a copper cast to her fair skin, matching the gold of her hair and her dry eyes.

Earlier the Royal Flight had been present; they had flown the body here and built the pyre. But as the fire snapped in its last moments, only the family of the deceased remained. It made brutally plain how few of us were left.

My mother and I held silent vigil until the last ember had turned gray and the wind had whipped the ashes into the sky.

When the silence was broken, my mother's words were even and clear, betraying none of the pain or anger that she must have felt. "Shardae, you're not to go back to the fields," she commanded. "I know your view on the subject. I also know you will be queen in barely a month. Your people need you."

Among avians, the heir traditionally became queen when she carried her first child. That did not seem a likely occurrence for me anytime soon, but my mother had decided it was time for power to change hands despite tradition.

"Yes, Mother."

I had been preparing to take the throne ever since my older sister died when I was ten, but my mother had rarely approved of my methods. I knew going to the fields was dangerous, as was visiting anyone outside the heavily defended Hawk's Keep, but how could I rule my people if I refused to leave the safety of my home? I could not know them if I never faced the world they lived in, and that included the spattered blood of the fields.

For now, I held my tongue. This was not the time to argue.

MY MOTHER LEFT before I did. When she shifted form and spread her wings, a black cloud seemed to rise from the cliffs above us, half a dozen ravens and crows guarding her even here.

I hung back a bit, hesitating on the black rock and repeating over and over the words

No time for tears. I knew there would be no energy left for living if I grieved too deeply for each loss, but each funeral was harder to turn from than the last.

Eventually, I forced the creeping sorrow back, until I knew I could stay composed when I faced my people, with no trace of anxiety on my face or grief or anger in my eyes.

As I lingered, a single crow detached from the rock above me. He circled once before returning to his post, assured that I was still here, standing strong.

There was nothing left to do.

As I shifted my tired human form into one with powerful wings and golden-brown feathers, I let out a shriek. Fury, pain, fear; they dissolved into the sky as I pushed myself beyond them with every smack of my wings against the air.

IT WAS LATE when I returned to the Hawk's Keep, the tower that housed what was left of my family, the highest-ranking soldiers and the most prominent artisans, merchants and speakers of the avian court.

With my mother's command, the seven floors of the Keep had changed from my safe home to my prison. Instead of being a refuge from the blood and pain, the walls were suddenly a trap keeping me from reality.

With Andreios standing near in case of trouble that never occurred inside, I lingered on the first floor, fifteen feet above the ground-level courtyards and training grounds. I watched the last of the merchants pack up their belongings, some grateful to have rooms in the higher levels of the Keep, but most wary of the world they would be returning to when they left here.

Market lasted from dawn to dusk. Merchants and storytellers would gather on this floor, along with common people, and during the day the Tuuli Thea and her heirs—her only heir, now— would go among them and listen for complaints. The artisans had nearly been strangled out of avian society by the war, but my mother had started encouraging the ones who remained to show their wares. The avian market was famous for its craftsmanship, and losing those arts completely would have been tragic.

Along with crafts, custom weapons and other fine luxuries, stories and gossip could be found at the market. This was where merchants, farmers and anyone else who did not fight heard all the details.

I had seen enough serpiente soldiers fallen beside our own over the years, and now, with the image of Gregory Cobriana branded into my mind, I was reminded once again that they were just as mortal as my own kind. However, fear makes all enemies more dangerous, and the stories told in the marketplace on this night were as sickening as ever.

Parents lamented their dead children. One young man broke down in tears, a display of emotion quite unseemly in avian society, as he recalled his father's death. Gossip traveled like a river: how the serpiente fought like the demons that legends said they had taken their power from, how their eyes could kill you if you looked into them long enough, how . . .

I tried to stop listening.

My people greeted me with polite words, just as they had the day before. Another hawk child was dead, along with a dozen of the Royal Flight, a score of Ravens—another flight, just below my personal guards in rank—and eighteen common soldiers who had joined the fray when they saw their prince fall. So many dead, and nothing had changed.

"Milady?"

I turned toward the merchant who had spoken, a metalsmith of good reputation. "Can I help you?"

He was wringing his hands, but stopped as soon as I spoke, his gaze dropping. When he looked up again, his face was composed. He held out a package carefully wrapped in soft leather, placing it on the counter for me to see. "My pair bond was among the Ravens who fell yesterday.

I had been working on this for her, but if milady Shardae would wear it, I would be honored."

The gift he offered was a slender boot knife, etched with simple yet beautiful symbols of faith and luck.

I accepted the blade, hoping I would never need it, but saying aloud, "It is lovely. I'm sure your pair bond would appreciate that it is not going to waste."

The merchant replied, "Perhaps it might protect you when you go out again."

"Thank you, sir."

"Thank you, milady."

I turned from him with a sigh that I was careful not to let him hear. It was already too late for either side to win; this war needed to *stop*. Whatever the cost.

If only I knew how to end it.

"Shardae?"

I knew the young woman who approached me now from when we had both been children. Eleanor Lyssia was an eternal romantic, with grand dreams that I wished I could make come true. The last time I had heard from her had been a few years before, when she had just been apprenticed by a seamstress.

My smile was genuine as I greeted her warmly. "Eleanor, good evening. What brings you to the Keep?"

"I'm finally allowed to sell my work in the

market," she returned brightly. "I was in charge of the shop today." The smile she wore faded to a somber expression. "I wanted to tell you ... I heard what happened yesterday. With Gregory Cobriana." She shook her head. "I know none of this is proper to say, but I like to think we were friends when we were children?" I nodded, and she continued, "When I heard what had happened, it gave me hope. If the heir to the throne can put aside the past and just comfort a dying man ... perhaps anything is possible."

She looked away, suddenly awkward.

"Thank you, Eleanor." The prospect made me want to laugh and to cry; I settled on a tired smile. I did meet her gaze; I hoped she saw my gratitude. "Fly with grace."

"You as well, milady."

We parted ways, and now Andreios moved to my side. As always, he knew when I needed to escape. His presence would dissuade anyone else from approaching before I could do so. I wondered if he had heard Eleanor's words, but we did not speak before we both shifted form to fly above the market to the higher levels of the Keep.

Andreios stopped at the fifth floor, where his flight was quartered; I continued to the sixth. I passed the door to my brother's rooms and whispered a final goodbye before I entered my own.

CHAPTER 3

I WAS A CHILD, UNVERSED YET IN POLITICS. The first thing that interested me in the court was a representative from the shm'Ahnmik, a group not allied with my mother, the Tuuli Thea. He was a falcon boy only a few years older than me, twelve to my eight. I was too young to know that my playmate made my mother very nervous, or that he was in the Keep for any reason different from the other children's. Too young to know that he represented an empire older and stronger than our own, without whose support we would never be able to keep our heads above water when fighting the serpiente.

I was just a child, with no responsibilities, no understanding of politics, war or pain. So I remember the falcon very fondly, as my last memory of childhood.

One of my tutors stepped out to speak with my mother in the hallway. "Milady Shardae, have you seen Andreios?" I looked up, hearing the name of my friend despite the tutor's attempt at discretion. "I'm worried that he's gone out to the field . . . to look for his father."

I was too young to understand death, but I understood that my friend was upset and so I had to find him.

I stood to sneak out before my mother returned. I had known Rei all eight years of my life, since he was three years old and I was newly born. He would listen to me more than anyone else. The falcon tried to stop me from leaving, but he had no authority over me and I refused to listen to reason.

My first breath of death hit me as I flew over the field. Yes, I knew of the war, but I had never seen the carnage up close, smelled the blood before . . . and in the middle of it all, my friend Rei, hunched protectively over his father's body, crying.

I landed at his side.

I hardly had a chance to speak before the serpent appeared. Rei pushed me behind him; they scuffled, and I saw the fangs slice into my friend's skin. Someone else attacked me from behind, but when I fought back, I was struggling with something as harmless as a wool blanket.

I realized suddenly that I was dreaming a scene I relived in my mind almost every night. I had been knocked out; Rei had saved my life. His brush with death had changed him, forcing him to grow up faster. After that day he had made a point of training. He had joined the avian army when he was thirteen and the Royal Flight when he was fifteen, and he had been the captain of that group for three years now.

Despite knowing I was asleep, I could not wake. Lucid dreams had been a curse of mine for years.

I walked the battlegrounds in my mind, through the woods and fields that I had been drawn to ever since Rei's father died. Pain, bloodshed, war. They had stained me that day.

I walked from the dream of Andreios to one of my alistair, the man who had been promised as my protector when we were both barely more than infants. Vasili had frightened me a little when I was a girl; he had seemed so cold and strong. The blood I saw in my dreams, he saw every day as a soldier. Yet I learned to understand him, and then I learned to love him—just in time to lose him, like I had lost so many others.

I pushed the phantom away and found myself face to face with the garnet eyes of Zane

Cobriana, the creature whose kind was responsible for every loss we suffered, every tear I held inside. My breath halted in my lungs; my blood turned to ice. I felt my throat constrict as I tried to scream—

"Danica, are you all right?"

I opened my eyes to find Rei searching the room for whatever had frightened me. His thick black hair had been hastily pulled back from his face as if he had been roused from sleep. He was not supposed to be on duty until this afternoon, but I was grateful he had been the one to hear me shout.

"Yes," I said, but the trembling in my voice belied my answer.

"Dream?" he asked. Rei was the only one to whom I confided my nightmares.

I nodded, sitting up. Morning was here, and if Rei was, too, then there was something important to be done.

Rei cleared his throat. "Your mother wants you to meet her downstairs, as soon as you are ready."

He left me to change, which I did quickly. My mother did not summon me for meaningless trifles.

I stepped outside my room to find the Hawk's Keep swarming with avian soldiers. In addition to Andreios, there were five other guards next to my door alone. Out on the field, I understood this kind of caution. Inside the Keep, it was unheard of.

"My mother isn't hurt?" I asked with alarm, my mind latching on to the worst possible reason for this concern.

"She's safe," Rei answered, though he didn't sound as if he was completely certain. "The rest of the flight is with her."

Of course. "Then why the sudden jump in security?" And, before he could answer, "And who in the world is guarding the outside?"

"There are about two dozen soldiers ringing the courtyard, and another few dozen in the surrounding land," one of the other guards assured me.

"They're good fighters. As for your other question," Rei answered, "we seem to have a visitor, which is why your mother requested your presence in the first place."

I had become used to having one or two guards at my sides, occasionally more if I was farther from the Keep on one of the fields. Having this many was unnerving, even though the Royal Flight were trained to work smoothly. They kept out of my way and out of each other's, but the press of their bodies in the hall was oppressive in itself. What kind of visitor required so many members of the royal guard to be in the loftiest halls of the Hawk's Keep? No one so much as got inside unnoticed. To get all the way to my chamber would be impossible.

My alarm jumped again when I realized that the guards who had preceded me had changed shape to descend to the ground floor. As a deterrent to flightless enemies, there were no stairs from the ground to the first floor. Aside from criminals and traitors, even the lowliest sparrow commoner was met in the second-floor reception hall.

"Who *is* this visitor?" I inquired softly. "Zane Cobriana himself?"

Rei did not joke back with me. He waited for me to shift into my second form, hastening what was usually a leisurely, pleasant process so that the hawk who emerged was more than a little ruffled.

My mother was standing with her back to us as we entered the enclosed courtyard. The visitor was seated cross-legged on the ground nearby, with her eyes closed as if she was taking a nap. Four of our guards surrounded her, showing just how afraid we were to have her near our queen.

Even from across the courtyard I could recognize the black hair and fair skin. As I went closer I saw her silky black dress with the white emblem sewn onto the low neckline between her breasts. On her left hand she wore an onyx signet ring.

Either she heard our quiet approach, or she sensed us some other way, for the visitor opened her eyes just then. Suddenly my cool, golden gaze was met directly by her hot flame, the color reminiscent of pure polished rubies. I looked away quickly, a shudder twisting its way up my spine.

"She's here in peace," my mother assured me immediately, but I could hear the "or so she said" in her voice even though she didn't speak it aloud. "Irene, may I introduce my heir and daughter, Danica Shardae? Shardae, this is Irene Cobriana, younger sister to Zane."

My skin chilled just hearing the name, but I answered the introduction politely. *What is this creature doing here?* I was willing to comfort Gregory Cobriana on the field, but he had been dying. Seeing Irene, alive and well and dangerous, I felt less charitable.

No doubt the guards had searched her and taken away what weapons they could—probably none, if this ruse was meant to gain our trust. But everyone knew you couldn't disarm a Cobriana unless you took its life. Their scarlet eyes alone were a weapon, not to mention their poison, which could kill in less than a minute if they struck in full serpent form, and which would kill more slowly but more painfully if they did so in a less pure form.

Irene Cobriana spoke first, for which I was grateful. If I had opened my mouth, I probably

25

could have caused a war with what I had said, if it had not been too late already.

"We want peace," Irene said softly, not rising. In case she tried to stand, the guards were prepared to kill her instantly. "We're tired of the fighting, and the killing."

Someone grumbled; I thought it might be Rei. My mother directed a frosty glare at someone behind me.

Irene also looked up at whoever had made the sound, and her voice rose with anger as she argued, "I have lost my father to this war. Two uncles. Three brothers. A few years ago, I lost a sister and a niece at the same time when some avian soldier put a knife into her belly and killed both her and the child she was carrying. My mother is a good woman, but she is only Naga, and the people will not follow someone who is only Cobriana by name. They need their Diente. And Zane is the last true heir to that title." Her voice quieted again.

"Excuse me if we don't completely trust you, Irene," my mother said simply. "But your kind has not been known to uphold its word in the past."

Irene lowered her head, and I could tell she was trying to speak around her anger. "Gregory Cobriana died two nights ago," she answered quietly. She looked at me as she said the words. "He was only *seventeen*, and now he is simply dead. I came here, without weapons, with the hope that someone might listen. Zane wanted to come himself, but my mother argued that you would sooner put a knife in his back than listen to anything he had to say. And do you know what he replied? He said, 'Let them. If they do, someone might finally be satisfied that they've won this war, and then maybe it will end.' "

I barely managed to hold my tongue in response to that claim. Zane Cobriana was what the serpiente called an Arami, the prince first in line to the throne. Now that his father was dead, he was all but king. It was hard for me to imagine the leader of the serpiente saying anything remotely tolerable, much less blatantly self-sacrificing.

Anyone who had spent enough time in the court had heard about the exploits of Zane Cobriana. In battle, it was said, he fought with single-minded fury, and a speed and grace no avian could match. He could catch the eye of his opponent, and that warrior would drag his knife across his own throat in a killing blow. He fought beside his people in battle and had never been wounded. Whispered rumor attributed his power to black magic and demons.

"And what exactly is . . . Zane . . . proposing?" my mother asked, hesitating for a fraction of a second before she spoke the name, as if worried the word alone would soil the Hawk's Keep.

"A truce," Irene answered instantly. "Zane, my mother and I would like to meet with you, your heir, and whatever others you think necessary."

"And just where is this meeting to take place?" my mother asked skeptically.

"Before the Mistari Disa," Irene answered softly. She took a breath and then explained, "The serpiente have been fighting so long, their only reason for continuing now is to avenge the loss of so many of their kin to avian fighters. They don't trust the avians, and I think it would take quite a show of good faith from your people to convince ours that the Tuuli Thea is as honest in her desire to stop the fighting as their Naga and Arami are."

I bit my tongue to keep from demanding just what kind of "show of good faith" Irene was suggesting. When she spoke, the Tuuli Thea said much the same. "I take it Zane sent you as a show of faith from your side," my mother said. "What is he asking in return?"

Irene shook her head. "Only that you agree to meet with us on peaceful lands before the Mistari Disa. We would like to appeal to her for support of the peace talks, and whatever is involved in those."

My mother looked at me. "Shardae?"

I started to object instantly . . . but then I remembered Gregory Cobriana's blood on my hands. I remembered the battlefields, the reek and the wail of war. I remembered my own alistair, Vasili, who had once been promised as my husband. And my own brother, who had been no older than the enemy he had taken with him into death.

So my words when I answered my mother were soft, but not without emotion. "I do not trust them, Mother, but if there is any chance that they might be honest, that Zane Cobriana might want peace..." I took a breath, because the very thought that Zane would ever waste a breath for peace was unnerving. "Then I believe we should take it." More quietly, I added, "You know that I would do anything within my power to stop this war."

My mother nodded. "Andreios, your thoughts?"

The leader of the royal guard paused, looking at Irene. "I don't like it, but Mistari lands are neutral territory. Even a cobra would be mad to try to ambush us there; the Mistari would tear the serpents apart."

"Very well, then." The Tuuli Thea gestured for Irene to stand and held up a hand to silence the guards' protests. "Irene, please relay the message to your... prince that we would be willing to meet him."

"Thank you, Nacola," Irene said warmly, informally enough that I saw a guard wince. She looked directly at me as she added, "Zane asked me to convey our willingness to meet any day, any time, as soon as is possible. Please speak a date, and I will tell my brother."

Again, my mother conferred briefly with Andreios, and then she answered, "In a fortnight, on the first showing of the moon. It will take that long for us to organize our people."

If the serpiente left the instant Irene returned to the palace and were willing to ride their horses to exhaustion, their party would probably make the deadline. The serpiente would not have time to plan a sneak attack before the meeting.

Irene curtsied, her face showing no annoyance at the rush my mother was pressing her people with. "Thank you, Nacola, Danica. My best wishes go with you both until then."

CHAPTER 4

M Y INSIDES COILED IN EXPECTATION OF
disaster as I made last-minute preparations
for our trip to Mistari lands. I knew the tigers
would not allow anyone to bring warfare to their
land, but I could not help fearing that this was a
trap—just like the one that had taken my father
from me. He had received a forged missive from
my aunt, who lived outside the Keep, saying that
she was dying and wanted her brother by her
side. The ambush had taken them both from me
in the same day.

Andreios had spent the two weeks all but
avoiding me so he would not have to face another
interrogation about the Keep's defenses, though
besides small, unplanned skirmishes caused by

chance meetings of our two kinds, there had been no battles since Irene Cobriana's visit.

It was only a matter of time.

"Milady? A problem." I turned, trying not to glare at the sparrow who delivered the message.

"Can it wait? We need to leave."

The sparrow shook her head. "The Tuuli Thea told me only that you need to speak to the Ravens before you leave for the Mistari lands."

Flanked by Andreios and five of his soldiers, I landed in the yard where the Ravens trained, a short flight from the Hawk's Keep.

The guilty looks a few of them tried to hide at my arrival did not bode well. The commander, a woman named Karashan, who seemed more sinew than muscle and whose arms bore many scars from her lifelong profession, approached me.

"Lady Shardae, to what do we owe this honor?"

"I was told there was some talk among your soldiers that I should be aware of," I answered honestly.

Karashan did not look away from my gaze, but she hesitated. "Well, milady—"

"Milady, thank the sky you're here," one of the younger soldiers said, giving a hasty bow before he began. "With all respect to my commander, the orders we've been given are mad—"

I could not hear the rest of his words over the murmur that started then. I held up a hand, shaking my head. "Your orders are to hold off, to defend the Keep if it is attacked but not to instigate anything. Correct?" I asked once the chaos had died down.

The commander answered, "Yes, milady. But surely there is some mistake? We'll be sitting here like lame turkeys when the serpiente attack."

I heard one of Rei's people fidget behind me.

My voice was calm, but my eyes were cold as I answered, "We are going to a meeting to discuss peace, Karashan."

The raven shook her head. "I mean no disrespect, milady, but I have been a soldier for seventy years. Serpents do not know the meaning of peace—or honor. If we do not attack soon and flush out whatever they have planned, you can be sure we will find snakes in our own beds."

I resisted the urge to glance at Rei in a plea for assistance. This had to come from me alone.

"Karashan, you have your orders. They come from the Tuuli Thea and have been repeated by her heir. Do you plan to obey them?"

She hesitated.

"Do I need to remove you from your position

to ensure you will not do anything foolish while my family is in Mistari lands?"

"No, milady," she finally answered, voice soft. "I will not give the order to attack. But, milady . . . if you do not let them move soon, my flight might not wait for my word. They are restless."

I nodded. "I trust you to keep them under control, Karashan. And if you cannot, I trust you to bring word to my mother or me before they take action. Understood?"

"Yes, milady."

I returned to the Keep feeling like a stone plummeting toward I knew not what. I ran my hands through my hair, trying not to look flustered in front of the Royal Flight.

"Shardae?"

I turned to see Karl, one of the few members of the Royal Flight who was my age, watching me with worried eyes. "Yes, Karl?"

"I will obey your orders as always, milady," he assured me, "but what if Karashan is right? You yourself agreed to go to the Mistari camps because there was a slim chance the serpiente might be sincere—so you, too, must know they probably are not. Isn't this too great a risk?"

I shook my head. "If they attack, we will defend ourselves as we have after every serpiente plot in the past. But if they don't, then maybe we can find a way to make peace. Isn't the possibility of your children never having to fight worth the risk?"

Karl nodded. "My trust is with you, milady."

I hoped I was worthy of it.

Before we could speak more on the subject, we were approached by the Mistari's avian representative, Mikkal, who had arrived earlier in the day to guide us into the foreign territory. "Are you ready to go, Lady Shardae?"

I sighed lightly, but nodded. "My mother?"

"She is waiting downstairs for you," he answered.

We joined the rest of our group: my mother, Andreios and two others from the Royal Flight. The Mistari Disa and Dio, their queen and king, had limited our number to five. We had been assured that the serpiente would bring the same. Shortly we were off to Mistari lands, with Mikkal in the lead.

The journey was not an easy one, even though my form was one of the strongest an avian could boast. The young goshawk was an extraordinary flier, and he set a hard pace. Once we had crossed the water and were over the sweltering Mistari lands, the trip was decidedly unpleasant.

The central city of the Mistari, if it could be called such, was surrounded by a natural ring of high stones. Inside those walls, the tigers of the Mistari tribes slept during the hottest hours of the day. Though the group had only been in this

35

area for forty or fifty years, since they had been driven out of Asia by the ever-spreading human population, they had already crafted sturdy walls where the granite mounds were too widely spaced or not high enough for their liking. Built into these walls and stones were the structures where the Mistari lived and slept, some grand and brightly decorated, and some little more than tents held aloft by simple stone piles.

In the center of the ring, one of the giant boulders had been carefully hollowed out and decorated with carvings of each Mistari leader, including the Mistari Disa and Dio. This was their simple palace—the reception hall, where we would meet with the serpiente before the king and queen of these people, and chambers where the royal family slept.

Our group was instantly surrounded when we landed and shifted into human form, but the natives relaxed when they recognized us. "The Disa and Dio are waiting inside the reception hall," a tigress told us. "The others are already there."

We were hustled through the tall grasses and toward the grand stone structure that was the heart of the Mistari territories.

Most of the Mistari stopped outside, but the tigress who had greeted us initially gently pushed aside the ornate silk weavings that hung in the doorway, and invited us into the hall.

The hall was more dimly lit than outside, but carefully cut windows shrouded with white silk let in enough light to show the brilliance of the Mistari palace. The floor was black stone, polished until it shone, and the smooth granite walls were decorated with an intricate mural of the African Serengeti. Brightly colored pillows formed seats on the floor, several of which were taken by the royal family's servants. Slightly raised on a red and black granite dais sat the Mistari Disa and Dio.

All of those individuals quickly lost my interest. Within moments my attention was locked on another group, whose members were seated on the opposite side of the hall from our party.

Irene Cobriana smiled wryly when I glanced at her, but already my gaze had moved on. Another woman, wearing dark burgundy, sat nearby. Her hair tumbled to her waist, a waterfall of onyx strands, and as she turned to look my way, I avoided her startling sapphire eyes. Charis Cobriana, Naga of the serpiente. The python might not have a cobra's power, but it was never a good idea to meet a serpent's gaze.

There were three others who sat with them, one female and two male. The first man was lightly built, with ash-brown hair cut short. The woman was slender, with blond hair that was tied at the nape of her neck before falling silkily down her back. They had the casual poise and obvious attention of guards. The male guard lingered near Irene, and the female near the man, who could be none other than the Arami of the serpiente.

Zane Cobriana lounged on a cushion, his back resting against the wall, one leg bent and the other straight. The iridescent shimmer of his black slacks led me to wonder which of his kind he had skinned. His shoulders were broader than those of a common avian man, and in the position in which he sat, the black material of his shirt was pulled taut across his chest. On his left hand I could see the onyx signet ring. For a moment he was absolutely still, then he looked up and unerringly caught my gaze. Twin pools of fire, a shade of red brighter than Irene's, held me tight. Time seemed to freeze for an eternity. Then his eyes released mine and flickered down my body, a quick scan that brought heat to my face.

Andreios had caught my arm. With a glare at the serpiente prince, Rei escorted me to my seat, blocking Zane from my sight.

We're here to try to make peace with that? I thought frantically. My hands were cold, my face still hot. If he could affect me that strongly from across the room, without saying a word, how would I ever dare to approach him civilly?

The Mistari Disa stood and held up her hands for silence among her own people. The hush dragged my attention away from the serpiente leaders and back to the Mistari queen.

"I already know that this isn't going to be easy," the Disa began. "But so long as both of you are willing to make an effort, there is always a chance for peace."

There was some grumbling between the serpiente guards, but Zane and Irene both shot them searing looks, and they quieted.

The Disa spoke first to the serpiente. "Charis, you are Naga, are you not?"

Charis Cobriana nodded, but then answered aloud, "I am, but my Diente is dead. Zane hasn't taken the throne yet, but you should address him as our leader."

"Zane, have you not taken a mate?"

Zane raised fiery eyes to the Mistari Disa. "Taking a mate in the middle of this war would be giving a death sentence to a woman in return for her love. I've learned from experience that even a woman with child is not safe from the killing, not when she's carrying a cobra's blood."

The Disa took a breath, nodded and then turned to my mother. "And among your people, Nacola, whom should I address as your leader?"

"My daughter," my mother answered. "Danica Shardae. She will soon be queen."

"How soon?" the Disa asked gently, and my head lowered. My mother had prepared me to take the throne, but I was still uneasy about the prospect.

My mother blinked and answered hesitantly, "My daughter has no alistair. The one she was raised with was killed in this war, and since Shardae is now old enough, I want her to choose her own. When I said soon, I simply meant . . ." She paused, then gathered her thoughts and answered honestly, "I am tired of this war, tired of being queen. My daughter still has faith, and if anyone is strong enough to lead us to peace, it is her. She will be appointed Tuuli Thea on her next birthday."

The Disa nodded again. "Danica, Zane, both of you have come here, asking for peace. Both of your families are willing to follow you. Why do you need our help?"

Zane spoke first. "Even if every one of us wants peace, our people would rather fight than be taken by surprise. Among my own guards," he said, glancing at his blond companion, "there is strong doubt as to how far we can trust the avians, and among many of my people there is even speculation as to why I would want to make peace."

The Disa looked to me next, and I could only agree with Zane. "We were barely able to control our soldiers these last two weeks. They don't believe the serpiente can be trusted, and unless we either give them permission to fight again, or we find some way to convince them that the Cobriana family and their people really want peace, my mother and I won't have the power to keep them from going against us."

The Disa sighed and looked at her husband. They conferred quietly for a few minutes, and then it was the Dio who spoke to us.

"You are both saying that your people doubt your sincerity, and the other side's sincerity," the Dio paraphrased. "You two are their leaders, and if you can set the example and show them how much you are willing to give for this peace, they will follow." He paused and then looked at me. "The question then is, how much are you willing to give?"

I thought about all the battlefields, all the dead men and women I had seen, all the dying children and fathers and mothers I had held and sung to. I thought about my dead alistair, Vasili, about my brother, Xavier, and about Gregory Cobriana begging me to stop the pain.

And I answered, "Anything."

A breath later, Zane echoed my response with, "Everything."

The Disa took over again. "When you have hatred, you need to start with the heart to mend it. Similarly, when you have a rift between peoples as great as you have, the only way to bridge the gap is to start at the center."

I glanced at Zane, wondering if he understood the Disa's advice better than I did. His eyes were narrowed slightly, as if he had an idea where this was going but didn't much like it.

"You came for our advice. All I can send you away with is this: You can only sew shut a rip by making the two sides one again. Danica Shardae, Zane Cobriana, you said you would give up anything, everything, to stop the war." She looked at me, at Zane, and then she spoke to both of us. "Never ask your people to do something you do not have the courage, or the determination, to do. If you want peace, start between the two of you."

The Disa spoke to the entire hall as she concluded, "The best advice I can offer is this: Tie the two royal families. Make the two sides into one. If you are willing to trust each other, and willing to put aside your anger and your hatred, then Zane Cobriana, take Danica Shardae as your mate. Danica Shardae, have Zane Cobriana as your alistair."

Andreios was the first to jump to his feet to protest, though the female guard shouted out not a moment after. Even my mother's voice rose, at the same time that Charis Cobriana stood. Zane's voice climbed above the others, saying, "I think that's an absurd idea," while my own objections were frozen in my throat.

Again the Disa held up her hands for silence, and one of the other Mistari touched Charis's arm and told her to sit. Another guard was doing the same to Andreios.

The Disa's voice was soft, almost sad, as she asked, "If you, the leaders of your people, are unwilling to make amends, then how can you expect your warriors to do so?" More loudly, she told the hall, "Stay here for the night, think on my words—"

Zane's voice interrupted. "Wait, please—"

"Dismissed, all of you," the Disa commanded. "You may return tomorrow at sunset if you wish to do so. For now, seek your beds, rest and think on my words."

Just like that, we were barred from the hall. The Disa and Dio left their dais as we were ushered out by Mistari guards and escorted to the rooms in which we would be staying.

A young Mistari girl brought water to wash with, as well as an assortment of cheeses, fruit and warm, freshly baked brown bread. I was grateful that the Mistari had thought not to serve meat, since like most of my kind I avoided it.

Rei stopped in to check on me once, and I had to assure him repeatedly that I would be fine before he calmed down.

He paused at the doorway and then turned back to me and apologized. "Dani, I'm sorry I lost my temper in the hall today. You know I care about you. I always have. The thought of that snake coming anywhere near you . . ." He trailed off and looked away from me as if he couldn't meet my eyes. "I should go. Good night."

"Good night, Rei," I answered with a bit of a sigh.

Then he was gone, and I was alone again, with only the flickering orange light of a solitary candle for company.

I lay back on the soft fur sleeping pallet and watched the light dance on the ceiling as I thought.

Never ask your people to do something you do not have the courage, or the determination, to do. If you want peace, start between the two of you. How could the Disa expect us to suddenly turn from enemies to a pair bond? She couldn't understand. The Mistari had never known the intense bloodshed and hatred our two kinds had known.

But still, there was a reason why the Disa was considered wise, a reason why warring people had come to her lands for hundreds of years when they sought peace. Never before had anyone managed to get leaders of both sides of this war together. If that was possible . . . maybe Eleanor was right—maybe anything *was* possible.

CHAPTER 5

A CHILL DOWN MY SPINE AND A FLICKER OF darkness in the corner of my vision announced his presence, even before the figure emerged from the shadows.

Still wearing black snakeskin pants and a black shirt that I now recognized as silk, the cobra terrified me just by being in the room. Pure primal instinct forced me to my feet. The back of my neck tingled, gold eyes dilated to catch every hint of light and every inch of skin was suddenly hypersensitive. My heartbeat had jumped instantly, until I could hear it as a near buzz in my ears.

"What do you want?" I asked, choking back a cry for my guards. Zane Cobriana would not be stupid enough to kill me in Mistari lands.

Would he?

I could not read his expression as he collapsed gracefully onto one of the large pillows that lined the room. "I decided that you and I should talk," he stated simply, his voice no louder than my own. "Sit down, Danica. I'm not going to ravage or bite you or whatever it is you're thinking."

I forced myself to sit, my legs folded under me in the fine linen slacks I had yet to replace with nightclothes. My heartbeat had slowed slightly, but I could still feel the pulse in my temple and at my wrists. "Talk?"

"We were thrown out of the Mistari hall quite abruptly," he explained, "and in all likelihood the same will happen tomorrow unless we have some discussion prior."

"Continue," I said slowly, trying to keep the tremor from my voice.

"Did you know there are four guards outside your door, Danica?" Zane inquired. My expression must have appeared surprised, because he continued, "I thought not. The Mistari added their own people to yours. They're all incompetent really, or I wouldn't be here, but it would have been tricky to catch you alone tomorrow. And since you're the only one in your group who has demonstrated any sense, you seemed the one to talk to."

"It's late, Zane, and I am very tired," I sighed, my unease and fatigue joining to make me impatient. "What is it you want to talk about?"

"About life," Zane replied lightly. Before I could speak, he went on, "And about death. About the fact that my people mean more to me than anything else, and I would do almost anything to end this foolish war. I want to talk about the world, and most specifically, about you."

It took me two tries to ask, "Me?"

Zane sighed heavily. "Of course you. If the Mistari Disa's proposal is even to be considered, I would like to know what I would be getting myself into."

"I believe you already expressed your opinion on that subject," I said dryly, falling back on the cool, distant tone of a monarch. I tried not to be a frosty queen to my people and my friends, but when nothing else worked, I knew enough to use that composure as a shell.

"And I believe my first reaction is probably still correct," Zane agreed, as if he had accepted a compliment. "It *is* an absurd idea, but that is no doubt why it has never been tried. I'm not saying I'll go along with it," he said hastily, before continuing, "but it does have some potential."

There were no words to express my emotions in that moment, though I am sure they bordered between pure terror and helpless fascination.

The Disa's suggestion was impossible. It would never happen. But still . . . "And what exactly do you think you are 'getting yourself into'?" I inquired distastefully. Before this conversation went any further, I thought it best to have some idea of where Zane intended it to go, since he had surely come here with some hidden purpose.

Again his gaze flickered down my form. "If it was just your body, Danica, I would agree very quickly," he stated calmly, and despite my fine upbringing, I was not ignorant enough to keep a blush from my face. He continued, sounding slightly resigned, "But one doesn't chose a life's partner for form, and the simple fact is that your mind comes as part of the deal—and *that* is a part of you that, despite years of musing over it, I have yet to fathom."

Years? I did not care for the sound of his phrasing.

"I thought I understood you, once," he continued. "Beautiful and arrogant and blind to suffering. And I had almost learned to hate you. But then I heard that the pristine Danica Shardae had knelt in the blood and filth of the battlefield and held my brother's hand and sung to him so he would not die alone. It made me think that perhaps you might have a heart after all."

I jumped when he reached toward me, belatedly recognizing the movement as something casual, a mere gesture while he spoke. His hand froze, as if he had not even realized he had moved until I reacted, and then it balled into a fist.

Zane was on his feet instantly. "Damn it, Danica!" he hissed, his voice soft but full of impatience. "I'm not going to hurt you."

I stood as soon as I felt Zane's temper, stepping back from the serpiente. Fear made my voice venomous as I responded, "Forgive me if I find it difficult to completely trust the man who has had so many of my kind killed."

"If I wanted to hurt you, I would have done it already," Zane replied bluntly. "I didn't have the slightest bit of difficulty slipping past your guards. Your avian heart beats almost a hundred times a minute at rest. Poison from a cobra's bite would reach your brain within seconds, so quickly you would never have a chance to cry out." His red eyes flashed with challenge, daring me to contradict him. "Trust me, little avian, when I say that if I wanted you dead, you would have been dead long ago. I wouldn't have bothered to set up this whole meeting with the Mistari. I would have broken into your room in the dark of night and smothered you with that Chinese silk pillow that you keep on top of the trunk at the foot of your bed."

"What?" My voice was very faint, with shock this time instead of fear.

I knew that he was only pretending to misunderstand when he said, elaborating, "You know the one I mean—gold and red silk, with flying black and silver dragons. Beautiful, obviously handcrafted—"

"Who told you about it?" I demanded, my fear jelling with anger to form a well-practiced surface of calm.

Zane raised an eyebrow as he collapsed back onto the cushion on the floor. "About the silk pillow? Or about the oaken chest it sits on?" He paused, raising his red gaze to meet mine, and I held it without wavering. "Or maybe about the white woolen blanket you sleep with in colder weather, which is as soft as new down, and the heavy tapestry that hangs across the open balcony doors in good weather."

My voice was lodged in my throat. "How . . ."

"I've been there," he answered simply. "I've seen it. The Hawk's Keep isn't the easiest place in the world to sneak into, but I have a talent for such things. I nearly got myself caught the first time, trying to figure out how to get to the first floor, but luckily avian guards don't often look *up* for an enemy. From there, there are servant staircases. You don't even keep your door locked, Danica."

I will now.

Finally he lowered his gaze, and I let out the breath I had been holding. "You're making this up." It wasn't possible he could have gotten by the Royal Flight. And no matter what time of the night, someone would have seen him in the halls.

"You really think so?" Zane sounded amused. "The first time I saw you, Danica, I was sixteen. I had just lost the first of my brothers in an avian attack. Someone—I don't remember who—told me you had just turned fifteen. For your birthday, my brother died." Despite the words, his voice remained calm, tired. "I rode a horse to the old Desmodus paths, and then cut through the woods. It was an hour or so after midnight when I found myself at your bedside. I meant to kill you."

"And why didn't you?"

"Sit down, Danica," Zane requested, in almost a sigh. "Do you have even the faintest idea how beautiful you are?" When I did not respond, he closed his eyes, as if picturing a long-ago memory. "You were fifteen. Only a year younger than I was. You were wearing white lambskin pants, and a blouse made of fur-lined cotton. I assumed you had fallen asleep before preparing for bed." He shook his head, opening his eyes. "I remember thinking you were as striking as the chaste Greek goddess of the hunt. I was young. And I wasn't a killer—not then, anyway. I had never killed before, and I couldn't start by destroying something so exquisite. I reached out to touch your cheek."

I was trapped in his story, trapped in the

cool voice and hypnotic eyes. As Zane spoke, he reached out, brushing fingertips over the soft skin of my cheek. His hands were cool but not cold, the touch as light as a snowflake's kiss. Even the contact of skin on skin, so unusual among my own kind, could not pull me from the spell.

"You cried out in your sleep and pulled away from me. And then I saw the cut on your cheek, right here. Your arm had another slice, like you had been in a fight." As he spoke, he traced the phantom injuries, which had long since healed. I suddenly knew exactly the time he was speaking about, remembering as if it had been yesterday: It was the day Vasili was killed. Only quick action from the rest of the Royal Flight and the defensive tactics Rei had taught me had saved my own life.

Zane's voice pulled me from my thoughts. "For a moment I wanted more than anything just to take you into my arms, but you had pulled away from me once already, and I was afraid of frightening you. I told myself I hated you." His voice remained gentle despite the words, as he trailed fingers through my hair. "But it wasn't true. You weren't responsible for the fighting. You weren't able to stop it any more than I was."

"Why are you telling me this?" My voice seemed very far away.

Zane spilled onto his knees, which brought him abruptly closer to me; my breath hitched sharply with surprise, but the way I was sitting kept me from jumping away.

"You didn't start this war, Danica, and neither did I," Zane stated. "It's been going on for so long it's meaningless; people fight because they don't know what else to do. People fight because their leaders fight, and then their leaders are killed, so they have more reason to go on." His hands touched mine as if he could not help but reach out. "Danica, my sister Irene is carrying a child. She was white with fear when she told me. It's an event that should bring joy . . . but everyone in my family just remembers an avian soldier plunging his knife into my oldest sister's swollen belly." I started to speak, but he put a finger against my lips. "No apology is necessary from you, Danica." Again the gentle caress of hands running through my hair as he explained, "I am going back to the royal hall tomorrow evening. My mother, sister and guards will not be there to argue with the Disa and me. I hope you'll be there, and that you'll listen to what she has to say. What she suggests . . . it might work. I'm just asking you to give the idea a chance."

Giving that particular idea a chance sounded akin to giving suicide a chance, and I knew Zane saw my hesitation.

"Please, Danica," he said. "You sang to my brother of peace and hope. I can't believe that you aren't as desperate for those things as I am. Just . . . try."

Somehow, I found myself nodding. "I will try," I answered finally, struggling not to think of how Zane knew the details of those long hours on the battlefield. He ignored my uncertainty.

"Thank you." He stepped forward so suddenly, his lips a brief, gossamer touch on my cheek, that I let out an unintended cry.

That shout, louder than our hushed voices, brought two of the Royal Flight instantly into the room.

Zane tensed, backing away from me as well as from my guards, and I could see his garnet eyes flashing as they looked for a way out. Insanely, I stepped between Zane and the Royal Flight, though Rei moved forward as if to stop me.

"There's no trouble here," I assured him, my gaze cool with the warning not to challenge me on this point. "I was just about to escort Zane out, anyway."

I felt Zane's tension lessen, but even so, the feel of him behind me made the feathers on the back of my neck rise.

"Zane?" I prompted, praying silently that he would not cause trouble now.

"Thank you for speaking with me at such a late hour, Danica," Zane answered smoothly, his voice as polished as my own, betraying none of the emotion of moments ago. However, his movements were cool and languid, almost lazy—dangerous. Everyone who had seen serpiente fight knew that they could strike as quickly as the snakes that were their second forms. They appeared so graceful and slow that you felt like you should have eternity to move, but you never did.

He was prepared to fight. Despite any noble words he might have said to his sister before she came to the Hawk's Keep, if the Royal Flight attacked him, he would fight back.

The posture almost made me refuse when he offered his arm, but his eyes still held a glimmer of hope, begging me to help him keep this from becoming a battle, so I swallowed my fear and forced myself to accept.

The guard on my side stepped back to allow us to pass, but Zane had to shoulder past Rei on his way out; the crow directed at Zane a look that would have wilted most enemies in their tracks. Instead, Zane caught Rei's glare, wrapped an arm around my waist and kissed me again.

I was too shocked at first to respond. In the time it took me to blink and Rei to stride forward with murder in his eyes, Zane had already stepped back, his gaze turning from Rei to me as he nodded a polite good evening, changed shape and disappeared.

Rei scanned the area around us as he demanded of me, "Are you all right?"

"He simply wanted to talk about tomorrow's discussion with the Disa," I answered honestly. "He was perfectly polite."

Rei looked skeptical, and the coolness in his tone as he asked, "Really?" reminded me that what he had seen had most certainly not been "perfectly polite."

"He was perfectly polite until you provoked him," I amended, voice hard.

"I see," Rei said, and this time the unspoken question in his words came through to me and my cheeks colored.

I turned on my heel to return to my room; childhood friend or no, I did not need to justify myself to my guard, and on this subject I would not do so.

As I walked into my room, I heard Rei say, "Inform the Tuuli Thea. Shardae!" he called, following me in. "Danica, wait. Please. I just did one of the stupidest things I have ever done: I intentionally got into a glaring match with a serpiente. And during those moments, he could have killed you. Do you understand? You might have seen a show of serpiente bravado from a fellow monarch trying to unnerve your guards. I saw him grabbing you, cobra fangs practically brushing against your skin, as I stood there *unable to move*."

I sighed, exhausted from the events of the day, frightened by how they were progressing and not willing to fight. "Rei . . ." I hugged him gently, a gesture too familiar for any avian setting, which made Rei tense for a moment before he hugged me back. It was nice to be in his arms and to abandon for a moment the reserve I was always expected to maintain. "Thank you for watching out for me."

"Danica—"

"I'm sorry I scared you," I continued, before Rei could finish whatever he was about to say. "But this time, you needn't worry about what happened. No threats passed between us—just talk. Two of us trying to figure out how to end this stupid war."

Rei nodded. "Danica, I—"

He broke off, stepping away from me and falling back into the formal warrior's posture as my mother entered, golden eyes cold as ice.

"Shardae, explain," she said shortly.

I resisted the desire to sigh in annoyance. "Mother, may we discuss this tomorrow? I would like some sleep before I need to speak to the Mistari Disa again."

"I would like to know what Zane Cobriana was doing in your private chambers," the Tuuli Thea responded.

"He came to talk," I answered, trying not to sound petulant when I was so exhausted that I was probably swaying on my feet. "He was worried that if we did not communicate first, the

57

meeting with the Mistari Disa would go the same way tomorrow as it did tonight."

"And well he should be. It was an atrocious suggestion then, and it will still be tomorrow."

"Are you so certain it can't work?"

My mother's eyes widened, and she lapsed into the informal in her shock. "Danica, you can't seriously be considering . . ." She trailed off. "It's impossible, and I won't allow it."

"I will be Tuuli Thea of my own right in a few weeks," I responded. "You don't need to allow me anything."

"For the moment, I do," she argued. With a glance at my guards, she ordered, "Andreios, get your flight together, and send the Mistari Disa our apologies. We will be leaving tonight."

"Mother!"

"Shardae, there will be no discussion on this point," she said sharply. "We are bringing you home if I need to have the Royal Flight hold you by your pinfeathers the entire way."

"What about the serpiente?" I protested. "We should at least—"

"Shardae, obey me!" To that final tone there was to be no argument.

My head lowered so she would not see the fury on my face, I forced out the words, "Yes, Mother."

CHAPTER 6

THOUGH I WAS INFURIATED BY THEIR RE-
fusal to listen to anything, I understood the
response my mother and guards had given to the
Mistari's proposal. In avian society, a young
woman was often promised to her future alistair
shortly after birth. The two grew up together, he
raised to be a guide and protector, and she raised
to trust him implicitly. He was expected to walk
the fine line of an avian gentleman, respecting
her strength and sheltering her from the harshest
of her world at the same time.

Vasili had been the son of two of the
Ravens. By virtue of his position as my alistair, I
was closer to him than any of my family or
friends.

Trying not to think of what I could not

59

change, for the next fortnight I threw myself into preparing for the position I would soon officially assume as Tuuli Thea. Those duties took up most of my hours, and when they lessened, I trained with the Royal Flight.

My mother had never approved of my being taught to fight, but neither had she approved of my walking the fields where the skills were necessary. Rei had long ago insisted that I learn some fighting skills, and now that I was restricted to the Keep, I used those lessons as an excuse to work off excess energy. Naturally, I could never best his people, but my skills were extensive enough to startle many members of the Royal Flight.

Half a month after our retreat from the Mistari, I was approached by a young girl no more than sixteen. She was slender and well built, and the fire in her eyes told me the question she was going to ask before she asked it.

"Shardae?" she greeted me, with the half-curtsy that was appropriate here. I nodded in acknowledgment. "My name is Erica Silvermead. I spoke to the Tuuli Thea earlier today, and she referred me to you. If there is a place available, milady, I wish permission to join the Royal Flight."

I gazed at the girl in resignation, not surprise. She was young, but no younger than so many of our warriors were when they began—no younger than so many of our warriors were when they died.

"Do you have any training?" I asked.

"Some, milady," the girl responded. As we spoke, I sized her up. Whatever training she had had was not formal, or she would have been standing at a soldier's ready, left hand gripping right wrist. "My brother taught me what he could." The unspoken words *before he died* hung at the end of that sentence.

"Follow me, and you may present yourself to the Royal Flight for consideration," I said, though I suspected this girl was of a lower class than the Royal Flight usually accepted.

Erica was a sparrow, a breed almost never admitted to the Royal Flight, since both their human and avian forms had a tendency to be light and unsuited to fighting. However, Andreios would make the final decision based on her abilities. If he thought her an ill fit for his elite group, there might still be room for her among one of the other flights.

Changing into my hawk form, I led the way down through the open circle in the floor and to the ground level, where the Royal Flight was currently sparring without weapons—a form of fighting that was an avian soldier's worst nightmare. My kind had the advantage of flight. If we were lucky, a battle could be finished with a volley of arrows shot from above. However, a clipped wing or lost bow could bring a soldier to the ground, where he would instantly be surrounded by an enemy who had every advantage.

Rei noticed my entrance and approached. I saw him take in the girl at my side. "Are you looking for me, Shardae?" he asked.

"If there is space to train her, Erica Silvermead would like consideration to join the Royal Flight."

Rei's brows tensed slightly, as if he was trying not to frown. "Silvermead . . . I believe I met your brother once, Lady Erica."

She nodded, keeping her head down a moment to compose herself. "You saved his life, nearly five years ago; he spoke of it often. I'm surprised you remember."

"He is quite a soldier, if I recall," Rei mused.

"He was," Erica amended softly.

"Ah." Rei nodded, bringing the conversation back into safe, neutral territory. "Come this way, and we'll see what kind of fighter you are, Silvermead."

He tossed her a blunted practice blade that, while not sharp enough to cut flesh, could cause plenty of bruises; I had earned enough of those myself during Rei's training sessions.

Erica's eyes lit up and she barely managed to avoid grinning.

"Try not to look so gleeful," Rei chastised

lightly. "Remember your goal, Erica: to protect your Tuuli Thea and her heirs, at the cost of your own life if necessary. You are a warrior. That means you will go onto a field someday soon, and you will kill another person."

Erica's gaze fell, but I could tell she was not overly daunted by the prospect of murder. Politely, she responded, "I apologize, sir, but one can hardly call serpiente *people*."

Rei nodded, not arguing. Erica was not unusual; this was a frame of mind most avians, children and adults, held strongly. However, Rei did ask, "If I bring you into a fight, can I trust you to retreat if ordered?" Erica tried very hard to hide her annoyance at the idea, but did not succeed. "I cannot allow you in my flight if you will not leave a fight when told to do so."

"Does this flight frequently retreat, sir?" Erica asked acidly.

Rei looked at me for a moment. "We are to protect Lady Nacola and her heirs," he explained, for what sounded like the hundredth time. "Frequently, that involves getting our charge off the field and out of enemy sights, and then following her. We are no good to the Tuuli Thea if we die for our pride."

"Yes, sir," Erica answered sullenly.

Her grin was gone, and her gaze was still down when Rei drew the knife from his side.

Erica reacted before the blade had even fully

left the sheath, and soon the two were in a flurry of attack and riposte that made my head spin in the attempt to follow. Rei was being cautious, testing his new charge, but I could tell he was using more effort to defend himself than he usually had to with novices.

To end the fight he got inside her guard and pressed the blade against her throat. Erica's blade was useless, trapped against her side.

She, however, did not admit defeat.

She passed the blade behind her back, transferring it to her left hand, and instantly it was against Rei's chest, the blade pressing just over his solar plexus.

"You're dead, Erica," Rei said.

"I'm not alone," she responded easily, slightly breathless, skin flushed with adrenaline.

Rei nodded, acknowledging the point. "You have some good moves," he admitted. "Care to try it again?"

This time he did not rebuke her grin; not waiting to recover, Erica returned her blade to her dominant hand and began the fight anew.

Rei did not check his ability in order to test hers, but while Erica did not have a chance to attack, she defended herself well.

As evening progressed, I made my way to the second-level court.

The market was peppered with gossips; the

court was filled with practiced scholars and speakers. Rhetoric replaced simple stories; ballads replaced the weepy tales. The serpiente's recent attempts at peace had already become legend, and the argument about what they really wanted was still going on. The idea that they had been honest was never considered.

After supper, the younger members of the court retired; had I not been heir to the Tuuli Thea, I would probably have been escorted out with the others. As it was, if I sat quietly I could hear the stories that the minstrels and scholars considered too indiscreet to share when the students were still in the room.

Rei usually came to court at about this time, mostly to call attention to me and hush the conversation when he deemed it inappropriate for his charge's ears, but tonight he was late. He sent another crow from his flight, but that young man had obviously not spent much time at court and was easily caught in the web of words all these speakers wove.

As I sat silently on the edge of the court, not in my place at the center table, people forgot I was present. Soon the scene in the Mistari lands was being discussed: how Zane had kissed me—scandalous!—in full view of two of the Royal Flight—shocking!—and neither one had made a move to stop him until he was already gone.

Though speculation about his motives and why the Royal Flight had reacted so slowly was a bit strong, the details were essentially correct; listening made me wonder how many of the other stories were true.

"Shardae."

I jumped at the voice behind my left shoulder, as did the guard Rei had sent to accompany me.

Rei dismissed the young guard with a displeased scowl, then simply said to me, "Considering how early you rise in the morning, I would be remiss if I did not point out to you how late it is getting." In other words, he could not order me from the court—he had no authority to do that—but he had no intention of letting me stay to listen, either.

Rei escorted me to my floor. Once, this level had housed all of my family: the Tuuli Thea, her pair bond and her sister and my own sister and brother in addition to me. Now, the empty rooms hung heavy with silence.

I bid Rei good night; then, as I had done every evening since our visit to Mistari lands, I listened to Zane's words over and over in my mind. Could he have been honest? I could not help fearing him for being the Diente, for the flames in his eyes and the fangs that were hidden but never gone from my mind. And yet I wanted so much to believe that he really wanted peace.

I slipped out of the slacks and blouse I had worn to court, and into my favorite cotton nightgown. The pale rose color always made me feel as if I was curled up in a sunrise. Small comfort, but I needed it.

CHAPTER 7

DREAMS SLID INTO MY MIND SO SLOWLY I had no sense of falling asleep.

Nightmare chased nightmare, until finally I was ten years old, on my knees on the crimson field, with two of the Royal Flight physically restraining me so I would not run to my sister's side. They tried to be gentle, but I fought tooth and nail to get away, ignoring the chaos of battle surrounding us—

I was dreaming, I realized.

My sister had died nine years ago.

Still, the smell of blood was so strong . . .

I tried to wake up, but only succeeded in throwing myself into another lucid nightmare. I felt a serpent's blade slice into my shoulder, saw an eleven-year-old Andreios—armed only with the bloody dagger he had taken from his father's still-warm body—throw himself at the enemy to protect my eight-year-old self.

I screamed as I saw the serpent start to uncoil to retaliate; I knew Rei would carry the scars from the serpent's fangs in his skin for the rest of his life, and I could not stop myself from trying to change history.

This time, instead of being knocked out, I was struck solidly in the gut by an enemy blade, knocked down with a choked cry of pain.

Vasili caught my hand, and though his expression was usually cool and remote, distanced as the hardest warriors always got eventually, he let me see past the reserve to glimpse the affection and concern in his nearly black eyes.

I was fifteen; he was seventeen. Vasili was not the warmest companion, but as he helped me to stand—not berating me for my foolishness in trying to find Rei's younger sister even though we had both known from the start it was too late to help her—I loved him.

I knew I was dreaming, but it was so good to see him again. I had missed him so much. . . .

And then he was twisting away, his hand going for his weapon as he pushed me behind him so that he took the knife that had been thrown at me—

Gregory Cobriana, clenching his teeth and looking away as he died, slowly. Rei, comforting as he could. I stood up as I had not done in real life and walked away. The dream phantom called after me, pleaded with me to stay, but I could not stand that again.

And then it was Zane Cobriana before me, twin garnets pinning me in place as he said, "Please don't scream."

Would I never wake up?

I could never have done so in real life, but in the dream I wrenched my gaze from his and shoved him away. "What do you *want*?" I demanded.

"I should think you would know that," Zane answered simply.

This was absurd. I wondered bitterly when this scene would turn to pain and violence like the others had. My nightmares had visited paths like this for years, one crystal-clear dream giving way to another until the morning, but until now they had always fallen apart the instant Zane Cobriana appeared. Now that I had seen him, spoken to him, my mind had more ammunition for nocturnal torments.

Zane watched me, his expression wary.

"You don't seem dangerous enough to warrant my mother dragging me out of the Mistari camps in the middle of the night," I commented to the specter.

The real Zane Cobriana terrified me, but this one was not overly intimidating. If anything, he reminded me of Vasili. He projected a mask that was numbed to pain, but beneath it he was as fragile and tired of war as only a warrior could be.

"I don't?" Zane purred, a glint of amusement now showing in his red eyes.

I began to pace. If I screamed and kept screaming, would I scream aloud? Would Rei come in and wake me? Or would the dream slow like molasses, as nightmares did, until it seemed I could do nothing but choke on the silence?

"Danica, are you all right?" Zane asked, standing now, too, the skin between his eyebrows tensing with the hint of a frown.

"Is there some reason I should be?" I nearly shouted in return. Zane winced, his gaze flickering to the nearby doorway. "I just want to *sleep*. I don't want to dream, because all I see then are the people I have lost. I don't want to smell the stench of death and decay and rotten blood. I don't want to hear the wet sputter of someone trying to breathe past pain. I don't want to see dying *children* whenever I close my eyes. But I am nearly Tuuli Thea," I said more quietly, "and once I am, that will be my entire life. War. Death. And I *don't know how to stop it*."

For a brief moment the arrogance was gone from Zane's expression, and he regarded me with what almost looked like respect.

"If I knew how to grant that wish," he finally

answered, voice soft, "I would have done so already, before this damn war had taken so many from me, too. Friends, lovers, family; I would have saved them all if I knew how. But if we both want peace, I can't believe that it is impossible to manage."

I caught him sizing me up, his gaze flickering down my form and up again. "Perhaps there *is* more to you than I see here, Danica," Zane mused aloud. "More than the stoic avian poise and emotionless reserve."

He reached up and ran his fingers through my hair, which brought him alarmingly close. His wrapping an arm around my waist brought me even closer, and then he kissed me, this time not hesitant in the face of my recoil or hurried to avoid a knife from the Royal Flight.

The sensation of his lips lingering over mine was startling; the light pressure of his body as he held me against himself was unexpected. He broke the kiss at the same time he pressed something into my hand.

"Tomorrow afternoon, Danica. I'll make sure the guards on the door are loyal and will let you in safely," Zane said, voice intense despite the fact that my mind was barely following it. I could feel myself sliding into the next dream segment, and I shrank from it, knowing the next scene would probably be a lot bloodier than this one. "We can't meet here in the open—your guards will kill me if they catch me—but I have enough control in the palace that we can make plans there . . . if you'll come."

I nodded, closing my hand on whatever he had given me.

He brushed the back of his hand gently across my cheek and then crossed the room to my balcony doors. I had a vague picture of him spreading wing and flying away.

Then I sat down to look at what Zane had pressed into my hand; before my fingers had finished uncurling, the scene changed and I was in the court, listening as Vasili debated some point I hardly understood but was willing to listen to simply for the chance to hear his smooth voice.

CHAPTER 8

I DID NOT ATTEND MARKET THE NEXT DAY; I was so exhausted I probably would have fallen out of my seat. By midday, however, I had been summoned from my room.

I followed the messenger up to my mother's personal balcony, the open top floor of the Hawk's Keep. There was a gentle breeze today, and my mother looked like a romantic portrait, noble and sad, but beautiful. She was dressed in raw silk, nearly white, with golden threads woven into the material around her throat, wrists and the hem of her pants.

The topic she wished to discuss was far from romance.

"Shardae," she greeted me, dismissing the sparrow with a delicate nod. "I have a meeting this afternoon with the flight leaders. This is the last assembly before your coronation, and I thought it best that you joined me." I did not have a chance to do anything but nod before my mother added, "Come, they wait."

Though I was capable of putting faces to names and matching those names with the flights they commanded, I knew very few of the flight leaders personally. Most of them reported to Rei, who then spoke to my mother or me if there was a problem.

Avian flights were designed to work autonomously, each having its own specialties and tactics. Rarely did all the leaders meet unless the Tuuli Thea called them to, and since the decision for me to inherit early had only been made recently, I had never joined my mother for these councils.

We descended to the second floor, where the courtiers had been cleared to make way for soldiers. At a center table sat avian men and women from all levels of society, all of whom stood upon our entrance. Beside the flight commanders, I saw weapon smiths and a few merchants who dealt in trade not discussed in the marketplace.

Around that table, I saw eyes that reflected horrors of every scope. Haunted expressions met my gaze as I was introduced in turn to each defender and necessary killer. The only commander I felt at all comfortable with, Andreios, was the only one missing; the commander of the Royal Flight would converse with his queen alone. In the meantime, his flight was surrounding the Keep.

"Please, sit," my mother said. The simple words began a conference I had no wish to be at.

Karashan spoke first. "Milady, we have taken advantage of these last weeks' lull to train soldiers to replace those lost fighting the cobra's people. We have also recently received a new shipment of am'haj from Ahnmik."

The concoction of which Karashan spoke, more commonly called avian poison, was a falcon creation that my people had never been able to reproduce. Aside from occasional fatigue, it had almost no effect on my kind. However, a blade coated in it would cause almost instant death to a serpent even if the wound was minor—an advantage we needed against an enemy who could blend effortlessly into the shadows and who was both faster and stronger on land than our soldiers.

Many times, the Tuuli Thea had petitioned the falcons for more than poison, as they were rumored to possess magic, in addition to controlling the most deadly soldiers ever to live. The price for that aid, however, was surrendering our freedom to the falcons and accepting subjugation in exchange for victory. Like every queen before her, my mother had refused the soldiers.

However, like every queen before her, she

had accepted the poison. It was the only way we had survived this long.

Karashan continued, "I believe the serpiente are feeling panicked, milady. The only incidents that have occurred since Gregory Cobriana's death have been easily put down." She paused, looking about the table, where others were nodding agreement. "We need to take advantage of this time, milady."

"I assume you have a recommendation," my mother said when it seemed Karashan was hesitant to continue.

"There is obviously serious disorder among the serpiente. I suspect that your early return from Mistari land may have interfered with their plans. Before they reorganize, I would recommend a direct attack. . . . We won't—"

"No." My voice cut through Karashan's. Suddenly all eyes at the table were on me, including my mother's, which were full of disapproval at my interruption. I continued anyway. "Doesn't anyone have even the slightest hope that the reason the serpiente have not attacked is because they honestly want peace?"

I saw the answer to that question before I had even finished asking it. The other flight leaders agreed with Karashan. I saw fear in some of their eyes, but more than that I saw jaded surrender. Peace was a *myth* to these people. They couldn't think of any other existence but war.

There was no way to change that here, and yet I wasn't willing to let them destroy everything, either. Trying to appeal to their more rational side, I pointed out, "We have tried direct attacks before. They only bring slaughter. If we attack the serpiente in their own land, we *might* strike a blow, but it will be at an incredible cost." Knowing it was a painful subject for many, I reminded them, "It took half of the Ravens, a dozen of the Royal Flight and eighteen others to kill Gregory Cobriana. And in the meantime, Xavier Shardae, my brother, was killed." More than one of the commanders looked away as I spoke those words. I knew then from what flights those final eighteen had come from. "That was on our own land. When the bodies were counted, we had two soldiers down for every *one* of theirs, including many of our best fighters and our prince. And you are willing to take the battle to serpiente land? Willing to lose a dozen soldiers to the archers on the palace roof before you even reach the ground? And then what do you plan, to chase the royal family through their palace?" I sighed, shaking my head. "It's suicide, and we don't have a hope of doing enough damage to end this war." Before anyone could argue, I added, "It's suicide even if they are as disorganized as Karashan believes they are. If you can't believe that the serpiente want peace, then they obviously have a plan. Attacking their heart would be walking right into it. As soon as our forces were destroyed, they would take the Keep apart."

Silence followed my words, a silence that was heavy with the weight of defeat. I didn't want to *surrender;* we would fight to the last sparrow before we would give up. But neither could I allow them to begin a battle that would destroy us—and any last hope for peace.

"Shardae, do you have another plan?" my mother asked.

Another plan? I wished I could have stayed in the Mistari lands to negotiate—no matter how frightening their first suggestion had been—but my kind was not trusting enough to allow another meeting. The only way I could speak to the serpents again would be without the knowledge of my people. Alone, I would be shot down long before I could even reach the palace to request an audience.

Stalling for time, I threw my only thoughts out. "Something less direct. Something they wouldn't predict." What wouldn't they predict? We had been warring for thousands of years, fighting like two dancers who know each other's moves without thinking. "If we want to attack them on their land, we need to know what we are attacking. But we've never even managed to get a soldier inside the palace—not one who returned, anyway."

"We need to do something," Karashan

declared. "Soon. I would accept losing every life under my command, as well as my own, if we could deal a wound that wouldn't heal. We've always been conservative in the past, and we've always ended up exactly where we started. Isn't it time to risk a little more?" There were murmurs of agreement around the table.

In some generations in the past, the Tuuli Thea had been ruled by this group. If I didn't make a decision, the chance would be taken from me, but I was not ready to set a date for the slaughter.

"I am accepting the crown in three days," I stated. My voice was strong, and it hushed the mumbling. "Give me that time to think. In the meantime, make your plans for the attack; it will take you at least that long to organize the kind of offensive you are talking about. If by the morning after the coronation no one has come up with a better plan, I will give you the word to go."

I glanced at my mother for her reaction; for the next few days, she was still queen. I saw hesitation on her face and silently prayed that she would abide by my decision.

Finally Nacola Shardae nodded. "Three days, when your Tuuli Thea gives the word." She did not mention considering other possibilities, but neither did she override my words with a command to attack now. "Karashan, the Royal Flight is needed here, so you will lead the attack. After my daughter's coronation, you will present the plans to your new Tuuli Thea for her approval."

"Yes, milady."

"Dismissed, everyone," she said briskly when no objections were raised. "Unless another method is decided upon, we will reconvene the morning after the coronation."

I watched the flight leaders leave, feeling shaken. After the three days were over, this would be my life. The battle that Karashan was talking about would be madness, but I saw no way to prevent it unless I could think of an equally decisive way to end this war.

When we were again alone together, my mother said, "You spoke wisely today, Danica."

"Wise words won't save people's lives if I cannot think of another plan, and I have no other plan," I answered.

The Tuuli Thea looked at me sadly for a moment. "I don't mean to hurry you, Danica," she said gently, her voice holding a rare note of affection. "But I honestly feel you are ready to take the throne, while I am long past my prime. It is a queen's faith that keeps her people alive, but mine is running out."

"You are young yet," I argued, upset by the note of finality in her tone.

"Perhaps, but some days I feel so washed away. You still have dreams, Danica. I have faith in *you*, and in what you can do. So does Karashan, or she would not have let you stall her plans today. She has been planning this offensive since Irene Cobriana first entered our courtyard."

I shuddered at the thought that different words might have sent us all to battle today.

My mother changed the subject to lighter things. "It occurred to me while you were speaking that when you accept the position of Tuuli Thea, you might also announce your choice for alistair. It would help the morale of your people," my mother explained.

I nodded, though with reluctance. This was her way of assuring herself—and the rest of our people—that the idea proposed by the Mistari queen was preposterous. "I will consider it," I allowed.

"Have you given any thought to whom you will choose?"

The question was just a formality, since we both knew the answer was Andreios. His lineage was almost as pure as my own, and as leader of the Royal Flight, his loyalty was unquestioned.

"I will be able to give my decision after the ceremony," I answered, thinking how very short the next three days were likely to be.

When she did not speak for a moment, I inquired, "Is there anything else you would like to discuss?"

She shook her head. "I wish I could have given you peace," she said with a tired smile. "Fly with grace, nestling." It had been so long since my mother had spoken to me with anything but detached civility, a queen to her subject, that hearing her speak so fondly made my throat constrict even though the words were a dismissal.

"And you . . . Mother."

After the words, I did not return to my room, but instead sequestered myself inside the library on the third floor. If I could not think of a way to reach the Cobriana peacefully, then perhaps these books of tactics and descriptions of past battles would at least help me think of something less mad than Karashan's plans.

Instead, I found a dusty copy of an ancient text written in the smooth, flowing symbols of the old language. Supposedly, the original text had been written by the brother of Alasdair, who had been the first queen of my kind.

No one could read the old language anymore, but when I absently flipped the pages, I found a few paragraphs that had writing above them—a translation, done by a raven named Valene. She had been a highly regarded scholar, until her quest for knowledge had led her to the serpiente. She had been exiled from the courts long ago, but apparently she had translated some of this text first.

> *My sister is a beautiful queen. She has seen only fifteen summers of life, but she has taken us from famine to abundance,*

*and transformed us from a poor village of
beggars to an empire to rival the falcons'.
They call her the golden one.*

A bit later, another piece was translated.

*Against my counsel, Alasdair has
allowed the serpents into the city. Their
reputation is not kind, and I do not like
their presence inside our walls. They say
they are only here to trade. My sister
insists they are as human as we are, and
should be trusted as we trust our own.*

A few lines were translated on each of the
next few pages, and then came the words I did
not want to read.

*In the back. She showed them only
kindness. She treated them only warmly.
They have nothing to gain. Trust a snake
to attack just because a trusting back is
turned.*

I shuddered, putting the journal aside. Was I
following in my ancestor's footsteps, giving trust
to a cobra despite every warning? Was I making
the same mistakes, to ultimately end with the
same fate?

CHAPTER 9

THE NEXT TWO DAYS PASSED TOO QUICKLY. Between preparation for the coronation and the looming war I felt powerless to stop, I had no time even for nerves . . . for which I was grateful. Neither did I have time to formulate a plan.

The morning before the coronation, I found on my bed two gifts, one from Eleanor Lyssia and one from the Aurita, a small shop run by a family of jewelry makers whose craftsmanship I favored but whose work I owned only one piece of. The family was too poor to be giving many pieces away but refused to sell anything to me at its full value.

I opened the package from Eleanor Lyssia and found inside a beautiful silken dress, the quality of which amazed me. The material was so soft it seemed to flow across my hands, alive, as I held it; the color was a beautiful burgundy that complimented my golden hawk's tones perfectly. I wondered how many hours she had dedicated to the intricate feather design carefully embroidered around the waist. Surely this was the work of the master seamstress, not the young girl I knew was the apprentice?

Yet there was Eleanor's signature, discreetly woven into the hem of the dress in matching burgundy thread.

The jewelry sent by the Aurita matched the dress beautifully. A fine gold chain suspended a garnet above the hollow of my throat; wisps of gold little wider than threads hung below the stone and made my skin seem to glisten.

The only other piece I owned from the Aurita was a delicate handflower, with similar fine gold chains trailing from a ring on my middle finger and across the back of my hand to a bracelet of twisted gold. The ring had been inset with a garnet that would match this, and as I recalled it, I decided I would wear that as well—if I could remember where I had put it.

Carefully, I removed the dress and laid it across the foot of my bed. The delicate necklace I placed on the nightstand nearby, and then I went to riffle through my jewelry box to find the handflower.

When I could not find it there, I checked my nightstand and the trunk that sat at the foot of my bed. Neither surface held the elusive hand-flower, but a brief search under the bed revealed something that glinted in the faint light.

I reached for it and then frowned as I realized it was silver, not gold.

As I pulled the ring into the light, it took me several long moments to realize what it was . . . and several more moments to convince myself I was right.

The stone was an oval of black onyx, inset in silver, and as I held the piece in my hand, I felt suddenly light-headed. The ring was heavy and larger than I wore—designed for a man's hand. It fit loosely on the first finger of my right hand, where it sat in satirical challenge.

I dropped heavily onto the bed, unsettling the beautiful burgundy dress. Without a doubt I knew that this was what Zane Cobriana had pressed into my hand, most likely intended as a symbol of his protection if I ventured into serpiente land. And of course, if this was real, if I wasn't dreaming now—and for a moment I hoped wildly that I was—I had not been dreaming then. I must have half-woken, roused by his presence.

I felt the heat rise in my cheeks as I reexamined my fuzzy memory of that night. I recalled my outrageous behavior and of course the neither brief nor chaste kiss with which Zane had ended the encounter.

He had asked me to come to serpiente land, and I had nodded; what had he thought when I had never appeared?

Dear sky above, he probably thought I had refused his offer to negotiate, his attempt at peace. After the fury with which my guards and family had dragged me out of the Mistari camps, Zane probably thought my nod had simply been a device to get him to leave, and of course he would not dare to return without knowing whether I had informed the Royal Flight of his presence. They would have posted guards on the servant's stair if I had mentioned Zane's nocturnal visits, and if he tried to return they would kill him on sight.

I knew what I would think, were the tables turned. For the sake of all my people, for the safety of the Hawk's Keep, I would be forced to assume the worst: that the serpiente were unwilling to consider an end to the war, and that indeed they were planning to retaliate.

Even if the serpiente had been sincere in their offers of peace, my lack of response would force them to attack before we could.

I could not afford to waste time.

Swiftly, I searched for suitable clothing: something that would not be ruined by a short walk in the woods but that was appropriate for meeting with another monarch. I settled on a soft blouse of woven raw silk the color of dark sage honey, and a pair of slacks of lightly tanned lambskin that would provide adequate warmth against the slight chill of the night. I reached for the boot knife the merchant had given me, but if I was going in peace I would need to go unarmed, as Irene Cobriana had arrived in avian land.

Unfortunately, I had no natural defenses to rely on, like a serpent's gaze or venom. I had wings with which to flee and hand-to-hand training that would never match a professional soldier's or guard's. A natural hawk takes its prey with talons and beak, striking too swiftly for resistance, and that is how my kind preferred to fight: from the sky. If I was attacked on the ground, any serpiente opponent would make it a point to keep me there.

Still, I put the knife aside.

There was, as always, a vase of flowers on the table beside my door. Remembering a signal I had developed with Rei when we were both mischievous children and I had constantly been sneaking out of the Keep, I moved the flowers from the doorway to the trunk at the foot of my bed. If he came looking for me, Rei would see the flowers and know I had not been abducted.

He would still worry, but this was the best I could do. There was no way I could ask him to come with me; bringing the Royal Flight would be suicide. Even if Zane had given his guards express orders to let me come with an entire regiment, no loyal guard would allow the cream of the avian army to enter serpiente land.

Taking a deep breath to gather my thoughts, I changed shape, luxuriating in the wonderful feeling of sliding from the awkwardly shaped human form into the beautifully streamlined, graceful one of a golden hawk.

Swift wing beats took me over my balcony, and within moments I was gone above the treetops.

I LANDED AND returned to human form several minutes' walking-time south of the serpiente palace. I knew there were archers stationed on the roof of the palace; if I tried to fly closer to the building, I doubted that even Zane's promises of safety would keep them from shooting me down.

Of course, Zane's promises still might not protect me on the ground, if he had even been honest in the first place. By this time, he probably did not think I was going to answer the invitation. If he had posted his loyal guards, the ones he trusted to greet me, he would have done so in the days after he had spoken to me. Now . . .

The woods were too quiet, and as I moved

through them toward the palace, gooseflesh rose on my arms.

"What do we have here, Ailbhe?" I jumped at the sound of the voice, and turned just in time to see a fair-haired woman step out of the forest shadows behind me.

Her white-blond hair was tied back in a loose braid, and her slender body was sheathed in smooth leather that laced down her back and both legs, tanned and darkened in a pattern so as to make her nearly invisible in the forest. Knives rode in sheaths on her thighs and at her mid-back, and a stiletto was bound in her hair. She also carried a stave as long as she was tall, the end of which was tapered and affixed to a silver blade. I recognized her as one of the guards from the Mistari palace and saw her eyes narrow as she recognized me.

Before I could move, I felt the sharpness of a blade at my mid-back. "What are you doing so far away from your flight, little bird?" a male voice inquired from behind me.

The woman stepped forward and nodded toward a wide tree nearby; a light prodding from the blade pressed against my skin moved me against the wood.

"Turn around," the woman commanded, and I did as ordered.

The guard behind me wore a similar outfit to

the first, altered to fit his gender, which I knew was the traditional uniform for the serpiente equivalent of the Royal Flight. He had the same striking white-blond hair as the woman, and features that suggested they were related.

"I'm trying to reach Zane Cobriana," I attempted to say as I turned. "He—"

The woman pressed the tip of her blade against my throat. "Quiet, hawk. Ailbhe, search her."

The man moved forward, and I tensed as he skimmed his hands over my body. The search was thorough; had I attempted to hide a weapon, it would have been found. As it was, the man seemed dissatisfied to find me unarmed. He ran his fingers through my hair as if I might have hidden a knife there, frowning at the feel of the feathers that grew at the nape of my neck. As he passed his palms over my chest, he found the pouch I wore underneath my clothing. I had hidden Zane's signet ring within it in order to avoid awkward questions in case I ran into another avian on my way here. The guard tucked the pouch into the bag he had slung across his back without looking into it.

I opened my mouth in another attempt to explain myself, but the woman shot me a glare that stilled my breath.

She spun her stave and struck me in the backs of the knees, smacking the joint with enough force to bruise. I tumbled to the ground, teeth set against the moment of pain, and the serpent addressed her fellow. "Ailbhe," she ordered, "tie her wrists." To me she added, "I'm tempted to kill you here, but Zane would be cross if I didn't let him interrogate you first."

With my wrists bound behind me, I was led by the two guards to the serpiente palace. Another pair eyed us dubiously at the front gate and followed my guards in.

Four guards for one unarmed hawk?

I remembered how Irene Cobriana had been treated when she had visited the Hawk's Keep, and realized that I was receiving the serpiente equivalent of that treatment. Did I really seem so dangerous to them?

I was led along winding paths I would never remember later. Finally we turned into a larger hall, but before I could take stock of my surroundings, one of the staves struck me in the back, knocking the wind from my lungs and sending me stumbling to my knees. Only Ailbhe's stave, positioned carefully in front of me, kept me from tumbling to my face on the mosaic floor.

Despite abused knees that protested the action, I attempted to stand, only to be struck again, this time across the shoulder. I bit my lip against the pain, trying to keep my chin up and my expression calm even though every cell of my being was screaming at me that I was deep in the serpents' nest and not likely to get out alive.

"Fetch Zane," the woman ordered one of the two guards who had tagged along at the doorway. He nodded and left the room without a sound.

She spun the stave menacingly, and I returned my gaze to the golden, copper and red marble that made up the snakeskin pattern of the floor. A few moments later the door opened, and the guard nodded sharply to one of the others to take her place as she went to greet Zane at the doorway.

Her "greeting" included sliding her arms around his waist and kissing him thoroughly enough that my blush overcame the ashen paleness of my terror; no one but me seemed surprised at the display.

Zane stepped easily into the hall, his hand lingering on the woman's waist with affection for a moment as he stepped away. "Adelina, what on earth is important enough to—"

He saw me, and instantly fury rose in his eyes; I flinched, waiting for another blow.

"Get your hands off her," Zane hissed, moving with the grace I had associated for so long with killing that my heart leapt into my throat and told me death was imminent. However, Zane dragged the guards to the side, tossing each inelegantly away from me.

Then his eyes lit on the guard he had addressed as Adelina, who was protesting loudly. She was silenced when Zane fixed his hot red gaze on her, cut off as surely as if he had held a blade to her pale throat.

Compared with the warmth with which he had greeted her, his voice made me shiver as he asked flatly, "Did you search her?"

"Yes . . . my lord." Adelina hesitated before using the formal, as if unused to it but recognizing that this was not a moment in which she should be familiar. "She had nothing."

Zane nodded, apparently unsurprised. "Out."

"Zane—"

"Out, Adelina!" Again Zane's anger, even not directed at me, made me recoil . . . and wince at the sudden spear of pain in my knee as I did so.

Adelina called to the others in the room, and the rest of her group followed when she left. For a moment I savored my surprise; had I told the Royal Flight to leave when Zane or Irene Cobriana was in the room, they would never have obeyed.

I jumped as Zane dropped gracefully to his knees in front of me. He drew a knife from his back, and for the second time in as many minutes, I was sure I was going to be killed; instead he reached around me and cut the bonds securing my wrists.

The position brought him uncomfortably

close. As I remembered the last time I had seen him, when I had assumed myself still trapped inside a dream, I realized that he probably saw no need for formality.

After the ropes fell away and I had turned to rubbing my wrists, Zane asked quietly, "Did they hurt you?" His voice was soft, but still rang with the danger I had seen moments ago.

"A few bruises," I answered, moving to stand if only to regain a semblance of dignity. "Nothing I have not—"

I bit back a rather unladylike curse as my knees went out from under me; they had stiffened in the last few minutes and were now protesting the blow Adelina had delivered to them. Zane caught me, and as I recoiled from him, it took all his grace to keep us both from falling back to the snakeskin floor.

The flash of anger in his eyes caused me to defend his guards. "They did no more than would be expected," I assured him, thinking again of when Irene had come to the Keep. "I assume they are your personal guards?"

Zane nodded once, still visibly simmering. "Their leader, Adelina, and her second in command, Ailbhe, are brother and sister—two of the fiercest fighters among the palace guards. They are also the last possible people I would have chosen to patrol if I had known you were coming."

"You had no way of knowing," I assured him,

attempting to cool his fury. "And your guards had no way of knowing I came peacefully."

Zane said dryly, "You are more generous than I am."

"Ailbhe has the ring you gave to me," I added, my terror having receded enough for me to remember that. "I had no chance to explain to them."

Zane's response was sharp. "Adelina had him search you?"

Puzzled at the question, I nodded.

Zane drew in a breath, then let it out before he said, "I'll speak to the two of them later. Now you should come sit and rest. You've been hit more than is good for you."

Catching my arm as if the movement was natural, he led me to the smooth oaken table that sat at the back of the hall. I remembered that he had offered his arm when Rei and his guards had found him in my room at the Mistari camps as well.

Touching in general was rare among my kind, even in such a formal manner. I had gripped Rei's or Vasili's arms some days when grief or war had led me to exhaustion, and that display alone had been frowned upon by most of the court. I had heard that the serpiente were freer with contact, but until now I had never needed to compensate for that particular difference.

Suddenly it occurred to me that I had no idea

exactly how far that openness extended. I recalled how Zane's guard had greeted him, and the kisses he had stolen both at the Mistari encampment and in my own room. I had thought at the time that he probably considered me either foolish or wanton not to decidedly protest such an action, but perhaps doing so was so natural to him, and he had not considered how shocking it would be to his avian counterpart.

Slightly soothed by this realization, I settled into the chair Zane offered to me, relaxing my aching body and cataloging my bruises. They were no worse than those I had gained in mischief as a child, or in weapons drills with Rei; the bruises across my shoulders and knees would heal quickly.

"Irene made me wait one more night before I decided you were not going to come," Zane stated as he swung gracefully into the chair opposite where I sat. His anger was slightly better concealed now, but it was still visible in the slick tone of his movements. "Thank the gods she did."

"As it is, I cannot stay long," I was forced to admit. "My guards do not know where I am, or else they would never have let me be here." *And if they knew how the palace guards had "welcomed" me, they would do anything in their power to keep me from ever returning,* I thought.

Zane's expression took on a hint of surprise,

and his voice was resigned as he said, "I forget how much power the Royal Flight has over its queen." He shook his head. "Adelina never hesitates to protest when she thinks I'm likely to get myself killed, but the guard doesn't dare try to stop a cobra from doing as he wishes."

Recalling how Zane had cleared his guards from the room with one word, I had no doubts as to the truth of his statement. Catching the glimmer of anger still in Zane's gaze, I was equally certain as to why the guard was so obedient to its prince.

"You're being announced as Tuuli Thea tomorrow, correct?" Zane asked, in an abrupt change of topic.

"Yes," I confirmed, slightly surprised that Zane knew the details so well. I allowed my expression and tone to carry the question, knowing that Zane would answer or not as he thought appropriate.

Zane caught the inquiry in my voice and explained, "I've people loyal to me who have access to the Keep. They keep me informed."

I swallowed a feeling of unease at the thought of the serpiente having spies in the Hawk's Keep. More unnerving was the knowledge that they would need to be avian, or else they would have been caught long before now. Zane might have been able to sneak around the Keep at night by using the stairway, but it would be impossible to follow the goings-on in the court without the ability to fly.

"And who are these ears of yours?" I asked, unable to keep the suspicion from my voice.

"If we manage to succeed in ending this damn war, I will gladly introduce them to you," Zane answered smoothly. Though he did not say it outright, the second meaning to his words was clear. If we did not end the war, he would keep his spies in place.

I had been aware that Zane's attempt at peace might be a ruse, but I had been willing to risk that on the chance that he might be sincere. It had not occurred to me until that moment how carefully Zane must have laid his plans before inviting the avian royalty to join this negotiation dance.

With painful clarity, Zane's earlier words reverberated in my mind. *Irene made me wait one more night before I decided you were not going to come. Thank the gods she did.*

If I had not come this night, would his spies have killed me in my bed? Or would Zane himself have done the honor, ending my life with the cobra's poison that he had once assured me would stop my heart more swiftly than I could draw breath to scream? Suddenly I was sure that if the time allotted to me had run out, Zane might have attempted to end the war by eliminating the leaders of the other side—namely my mother and me—with methods far more sure than any of Karashan's plans.

As if reading my thoughts in the silence I allowed to pass, Zane stated coolly, concisely, "If I give you my word, Danica, you can be assured I will keep it. I want bloodshed no more than you do, but I will do what is necessary to end this war. If that means accepting the Mistari's suggestion, then I will go down on bended knee this moment and ask you to be my Naga. If that means listening to any other suggestion you have . . . so be it." He concluded, his tone never changing, "And if it means taking the Hawk's Keep down stone by stone with my bare hands, then without hesitation I will begin."

I stood, moving away from the intensity in his gaze. If I refused to listen . . . would I even be allowed to leave?

"I came here to talk about peace, not to receive threats."

"I gave my word you would be safe if you accepted my invitation," Zane assured me, not rising from his seat, as if attempting the impossible feat of appearing harmless. "If you turned around right now and left, neither my guard nor I would stop you."

"And afterward?"

Zane closed his eyes for a moment, and when he opened them again his expression was as remote as the morning star. "I hope we can end this war with peace, not a bloodbath," he answered. "I've reached the point where I honestly think I would slit my own wrists if I thought it would end the fighting. Unfortunately, the palace guard would not react well to losing its last prince, and again we would have a slaughter on our hands." He shook his head and finished bluntly, "You are an attractive woman, Danica, but I do not love you. I do not think I ever can. I look into your golden hawk's eyes, and no matter how stunning the form they accompany, I think only of your warriors murdering my loved ones. Since you recoil every time you accidentally find your own gaze fallen upon Cobriana garnet, I suspect you feel much the same way."

"Are these statements going somewhere?" I inquired, voice detached.

"I wanted to make sure there were no misunderstandings between us before I asked my next question," Zane answered immediately. He stood, and I braced myself to keep from flinching as he moved toward me. "I have considered our options, and elected to attempt the least bloody first." Graceful as the serpent that lived inside him, Zane went down on one knee. "With the understanding that there may never be anything between us but a shared desire for peace, and my word that I will never force upon you any duty beyond the political expectations of the position,

I implore you, Danica Shardae, to agree to be my Naga."

I felt my heart skip a beat, and for several seconds my voice caught in my throat.

He couldn't want an answer now . . . but of course he did, or he would not have asked. Zane waited silently, still as a statue, as I alternated between animalistic terror, the desire to flee, acceptance of my responsibilities and the knowledge that if I said no now, I would need to return to the council and prepare for battle.

How could I possibly *consider* saying yes when I knew that with as little hesitation as he had gone to one knee, Zane could stand and slip a knife between my ribs?

How could I consider saying no, when agreeing now might end this war?

"I don't know how in the world I could convince my protectors to back my decision," I admitted, and my voice was nearly shaking. The rest of the council would follow the Royal Flight, but I felt certain that Andreios would be the first to protest my endangering myself with this agreement.

"Yes or no is all that matters," was Zane's swift response. "We'll work out the details later."

I took a breath, felt my throat constrict and had to swallow hard twice before I could answer, "Yes. I agree."

·Zane stood, catching my right hand as he did so. He laid a gentle kiss on my knuckles, then turned it over and pressed another ring into my palm.

The style matched the Cobriana signet ring, though this one was smaller, designed to fit my slender fingers. The metal was the same cool silver, but instead of the traditional black stone, this had been set with a rare golden onyx, with bands varying from pale honey to warm marigold. I knew it must have come from the Mistari's original homeland in the east.

"I have informed my people that I will announce my Naga on the new moon—two nights from now. I know it is the evening after your coronation as Tuuli Thea, and if necessary I can push it back, but it seems wise to make our move as soon as we can."

I nodded, and as it occurred to me, I added, "There will be protests, but if we go through with the announcement here before I inform the court of my decision, not only will I have the title of Tuuli Thea behind me, but it will be too late for even the Royal Flight to forbid me. It is a high crime for an alistair's vows to be broken." No one would dare order the Tuuli Thea to withdraw her promise, even if it was given to the Diente of the serpiente. I could stall picking an alistair easily enough, though it would be trickier to bluff Karashan into delaying. But it would only be a

few days, long enough to seal the pact on the serpiente side; I would do it, whatever it took.

"How are your people likely to take the
news?" I asked hesitantly. My main concern was
that someone might attempt to kill Zane if I
tried to take him to the Keep and acknowledge
him as my alistair; I hoped I would not be dodg-
ing weaponry when Zane made the announcement here.

"They won't like it; they'll think I'm more
than a little crazy. There will be those who will
worry you are going to put a knife in me one
night, and some who will think a strange avian
magic has twisted my mind," Zane answered easily. "But you're beautiful, and there's no reason
for them to think I'm not madly infatuated even
if you are a hawk. That being so, they frankly
cannot afford to take the announcement badly.
One can be skinned for harming the Naga or her
personal guards, which for you will include the
Royal Flight. They'll be wary of picking fights
with avian soldiers, at least for a while."

Skinned? I shuddered at the thought, though I
certainly did agree that such a threat would be a
strong deterrent to anyone intending harm.

I nodded, accepting Zane's reasoning. "I need
to get back to the Keep before the Royal Flight
comes looking for me," I stated, lifting my
bruised body carefully from my seat.

"Can you be here at about midday after the

ceremony at the Keep?" Zane asked. "That will leave some time to prepare you for meeting the serpiente court." The concept of standing in front of a large group of hostile serpiente, relying only on the promise of Zane Cobriana to keep me safe, made my blood run cold.

"That should be fine," I responded, my voice sounding distant to my ears. I almost felt like I was dreaming again, but even my mind could not have created a scenario as terrifying as this one.

CHAPTER 10

B Y THE TIME I RETURNED TO THE KEEP, IT
was nearly dawn, yet I had barely returned to
human form before Andreios was standing before
me and demanding to know where I had been.

I used the pretense of catching my breath as I
thought quickly and finally settled for the closest
thing to the truth I could manage. "When I spoke
to the flight leaders, I mentioned the possibility
of a less direct solution. I have been finalizing the
details of that solution." Rei's eyes widened as I
continued, "I have a plan, but it is discreet. In the
meantime, I want you to tell the flight leaders to
stand down. I don't want a move made beyond
what I have already triggered. I plan ... to turn
the serpiente's plot back upon them."

I knew all the ways he could take the words,

and I knew he would never translate them to mean that I had agreed to go along with Zane Cobriana's plans. Karashan thought the serpiente were standing down to draw us into a trap. Let her think I was using the same plan.

"Are you sure?" was all Rei asked.

I wanted to tell him the full truth, but revealing the real plans would ruin them. Neither my mother nor the Royal Flight would let me get away with this madness.

That very fact was what tempted me the most. If I told them and they stopped me from going through with the insane agreement I had made with a cobra, I could tell myself that it wasn't my fault. At least until I walked the next bloody battlefield, or took the throne and, like my mother, lost children to the war. The first blood I saw would be on my hands, as would any spilled afterward.

I kept my fears to myself. "I am sure," I said. "Give Karashan the orders: not a move."

He nodded, and we parted ways. I returned to my bed to get some much-needed rest before the coronation that evening.

The ceremony was simple: a few words spoken to the court by my mother of my strength and courage and faith in the future, words that felt hollow in my ears as terror beat in my heart. From her own neck my mother removed a pendant of a golden hawk with wings spread, a solitary symbol on the end of a carefully woven gold and silver chain. I was wearing the necklace the Aurita had given to me; the piece hung high enough that I could wear the hawk pendant at the same time, so that each decoration seemed made to wear with the other.

I addressed my people, and saw my mother frown when I finished without speaking of my alistair. However, it was not until the Royal Flight knelt before me to swear their allegiance to the new Tuuli Thea that the horror of what I had promised Zane was made real to me.

"Gerard Halsan." Speaking his name, the older man knelt before me, taking my hand and speaking the words he had recited when he had sworn his allegiance to my mother before me. "To my Tuuli Thea goes my faith and my trust. To her blood goes my blade, my bow and my fist, ever to defend her and her kin. To her I swear my loyalty, and to her I swear my life ever before hers."

My life ever before hers. These two dozen men and women, their lives before mine. I prayed they would never need to give those lives. I prayed I could stop the war before they were called to sacrifice themselves for another helpless queen.

I knew every name and face among the Royal Flight. Some of them, like Karl and Andreios, I had grown up with; some of them, like Gerard, had guarded my mother before I was even born.

The list went on, coming at last to Erica

Silvermead. The newest member of the Royal Flight, the low-born sparrow who had shocked Andreios with her ability. If I had to guess, her name would be high on my list of Zane's possible spies; she had come out of nowhere. But I knew the assessment was not quite fair. Erica had barely been accepted into the Royal Flight, and she had only been in the Keep for a few days; Zane had implied that his spies had been in place for a while. There was just something about the sparrow that unnerved me. However, Rei seemed very proud of how well she fought, so I did not speak my unease. As Erica swore her vows, her voice rang sincere.

The last to stand before me was the commander of the Royal Flight himself.

Andreios stood respectfully, but in his eyes was a look akin to pain, a question he would not ask. Still, he smiled at me as he approached and went to his knee.

"To my Tuuli Thea goes my vow to train those under me, to lead them well, so our wings may be hers if she falls, so our eyes may be hers in darkness, and our talons may be hers in danger. To her blood goes my blade, my bow and my fist, ever to defend her and her kin. To her I swear my trust and my loyalty. To her I swear my life ever before hers."

He took my hand and kissed the back of it. The movement was formal, but I wished it was not. I had sworn myself to another man, a cobra, and left Rei to wonder what had happened to keep me from naming him my alistair today as we had assumed I would.

THE RECEPTION AFTER the coronation and the vows was a farce. Every member of the avian court approached me with congratulations and words of advice, and to all of them I wanted to say, "Do you know what I have done? What I am going to do?"

My mother approached me as soon as I had a moment of peace. She offered no words of congratulations, but said, "You decided not to choose your alistair tonight?" The words asked many things.

I had practiced my half-lies since speaking to the council, and when I answered, my voice was polished. "We spoke a few days ago of acting in this war. I have been working with a select few on a plan that I hope will be less bloody than sending scores of soldiers into enemy territory." I saw a moment of surprise in my mother's face and continued. "I would like, when I announce my alistair, to announce with him a new reign of peace. I would like to announce that Zane Cobriana no longer stands as our enemy. And I intend to."

Skepticism was not hidden from my mother's voice as she asked, "What is this plan?"

"Wait, Mother," I answered with a sigh. "I will announce the outcome . . . in three days' time, in front of the court. I will announce my alistair then. Until then, I will hear no questions."

I knew she wanted to ask, but she held her tongue. I was Tuuli Thea now; she had no power to challenge me.

It was nearly midnight when I managed to sneak out to the balcony for a breath of fresh air. I leaned against the railing, staring at the line where the treetops met the starlit sky.

I was not alone long. Andreios joined me, not speaking but giving me a chance if I wanted it. I only wished I knew what to say.

I started to turn away, but his voice drew me back. "Danica?"

His features were shadowed, but not enough to hide the look of determination on them.

"It's all right," he said, voice gentle. "I understand. I love you, and I always have. What matters to me is that you are happy. If there's someone else, I wish you luck with him." My heart raced at his words. I opened my mouth to say *There's no one else*, but of course there was—a serpent. "And if you're just not ready, I can wait."

I was unwilling to lie, but couldn't tell him the truth. I reached out to him, and he caught my hand and kissed the back of it. I remembered Zane doing the same so recently and couldn't speak. Words of love seemed cruel when the next night I would pledge myself to another man.

The words I uttered were halting but honest. "You have been a friend to me ever since we were children." I saw him flinch at the words, but continued, "There is no one I trust more. No one I care for more. But . . ." I shook my head. "It's impossible to explain."

I saw a sudden hint of fear and suspicion in his eyes and turned away before he could speak again. I returned to my room and collapsed into bed, where I stared at the ceiling and tried to block my own fears from my mind.

I WOKE A few hours after sunrise. Yawning, I dragged myself out of bed and called for a cold bath to try to rouse myself.

The hawk pendant was still around my neck, and I lifted it to examine the intricate detail of the wings and eyes.

Tuuli Thea. Though I had been preparing for the title since my sister's death, the position still seemed unreal. The idea that I was now the one the Royal Flight would look to, the one who would hear complaints of the common people in the market and the one who would be expected to administer justice in response to a crime seemed impossible.

And by tomorrow, the title will be Naga as well. I did not wish to dwell on that prospect, but of course I was forced to as I took my bath and the cold water woke my mind and my fears.

The dress I had worn for the ceremony the day before had been aired and hung. Though the flowing skirt, decent neckline and low back designed to allow the Demi form's wings to grow if it became necessary was an avian style, the warm burgundy and soft silk reminded me of the outfits I had seen Irene and Charis wear. It would be perfect for the ceremony at the palace. I laid it out with a silent thanks to Eleanor, its creator.

Struggling into the complicated garment alone might prove difficult; a maid had helped me with several of the clasps in the back the first time. But I would manage.

The next problem was a slightly larger one.

I could not simply disappear all day and evening without exciting a panic among the Royal Flight.

I drafted a letter, though I knew leaving a note in my room was a rather guilty way of avoiding confrontation. I also worried that someone might find it too early. I needed someone who could cover for me for a few hours and then explain to the Royal Flight where I had gone.

Eleanor. Might she be of help? She was more open-minded than most of the court, and might be willing to be my intermediary. I summoned her to my drawing room and paced on the balcony as I waited for her to appear.

"I need a favor from you," I stated once the woman was present and the page-in-training who had brought her was gone.

"What would you like?" she answered easily, unsuspicious.

"I have been conducting negotiations with the serpiente," I explained, leaving out all specifics and watching her face carefully for signs of revulsion. Eleanor appeared startled, but did not immediately reject the idea. "The Royal Flight does not know what my plans are, but I am worried I will be missed while I am away today—"

"Won't they expect you to be at market for Festival?" Eleanor asked with wide-eyed faux innocence. "I know it's supposed to be a day for merchants and children, but I've never in my life known you or any of the royal family to miss it."

In the recent days' mixture of confusion and tension, I had honestly forgotten about Festival, which occurred about two months before midsummer. Every year, market was filled to bursting with magicians, storytellers and other entertainers. Though the Tuuli Thea and her heirs were traditionally not a part of the celebrations, I had always loved the bright decorations and beautiful songs that accompanied them. Even the Royal Flight let its guard down, as it was unlikely that anyone would manage to harm the heir to the Tuuli Thea among such a press of her subjects.

"Perfect," I breathed. "Andreios won't be surprised if he doesn't see me until nearly sunrise." Pacing with nervous excitement, I asked, "Eleanor, would you be able to deliver a message to the Royal Flight? I might be back before they even miss me, but if not, Andreios should be informed of my whereabouts."

Eleanor nodded. "I can do that. Festival will last until sunrise. If I have not heard from you by then, I can speak to your protector."

"Thank you." I read over my letter one more time before sealing it and entrusting it to the seamstress.

Eleanor's gaze moved to the burgundy dress that I had not yet donned to replace the simple outfit I was wearing for the morning, and I saw her smile a little. "I know the design on that is a little complicated. Do you need help?"

"Eleanor, you are a goddess," I breathed. So far, this venture was falling into place easily—too easily. It was beginning to worry me.

Dressed and ready, I gave one last look to the letter Eleanor held. It was a concise explanation of my conversations with Zane Cobriana to date, as well as where I would be that evening, and why. *If you wish to seek me,* the letter continued,

I recommend that you do so peacefully. I want this ceremony to proceed without bloodshed, and you are enough of a soldier to know that Zane's people will not respond well if your flight appears fully armed at the palace. I do not know what serpiente tradition expects of this ceremony; I will return as soon as is seemly.

The letter was signed and sealed, and it would be delivered. Now all that was left was to make the words true.

MY GREETING AT the serpiente palace was much gentler this time, and it came in the form of a trio of young female guards. They said little, and while their gazes alternated between distaste and curiosity, I was neither searched nor struck, for which I was grateful beyond belief.

Once again I was led through the twisting maze of the serpiente palace, and though I tried to memorize the turns we took and the doors we passed through, I found it impossible to do so. I was glad I was a willing guest and not a prisoner trying to escape; one could probably wander these halls for hours without finding anyplace familiar.

A tendril of curiosity rose. In the past, I never could have imagined exploring the inside of the serpiente palace, which was described as a labyrinth of halls and secret passages. Now, I might have a chance.

I recognized the large honey-oak double

doors before my escort pushed them open to reveal the hall where I had met Zane the first day I had come here.

Zane was pacing anxiously, while Irene and Charis Cobriana were seated at the large table that dominated the far side of the room. Now Zane dismissed the three guards with a word and greeted me warmly.

"Danica, allow me to introduce Naga Charis Cobriana," he first began formally. "And you have met my sister, Irene."

"A pleasure to meet you." I was very proud of myself; my voice did not shake as I greeted the present Naga of the serpiente, Zane's mother.

I also forced myself to meet her gaze as I spoke, as was polite; Charis did not attempt to hold my eye. "My son speaks quite highly of you." There was some laughter in her voice, as if Zane's speaking "quite highly" might have been intermixed with his speaking quite lowly, but considering I had been on pins and needles lately, I could only imagine how Zane had been around his family.

"How shortly should I expect your guards to storm the palace?" Zane asked, his voice also holding an amused lilt that did not manage to completely cover the more serious thoughts beneath.

"The Royal Flight will be informed of my whereabouts shortly before sunrise, if I have not returned by then," I answered, my voice as light as his despite my nervousness.

One of the hall's double doors opened partially and Adelina entered. She nodded deferentially to Charis and Irene, then said, "Zane, you are needed."

"Am I?" Zane's voice was clipped, not cold but short with tension. "I'd like to know what your guard needs me for at this moment."

"*I* need to speak to you," she amended, with a look to kill directed at me.

"You can speak as freely in front of Danica as you can in front of me," Zane assured her.

A moment of awkward silence followed, stretching until Irene stood and put a hand on Zane's arm. The cobra caught Zane's eye and nodded sharply in Adelina's direction, a silent command. "She deserves a chance to speak with you before the ceremony. Mother and I will prepare Danica."

Zane hesitated, but finally led the way out of the room. They paused in the hall, and Adelina closed the door.

"She knows not to hit anywhere the bruises will show, right?" Charis asked lightly.

Irene smiled wryly. "She knows—though I doubt Zane's in a mood to tolerate it even if she is justified."

"Is there something I'm missing here?" I asked worriedly. The implication that Zane's own guard might harm him was rather unpleasant.

It occurred to me again that there were reasons beyond history behind why the serpiente and the avians were at war. If a member of the Royal Flight raised a hand to my family or me, he or she would be ostracized to human society, feathers shorn, grounded forever. Yet Charis and Irene were discussing the possibility of Adelina's striking Zane as if it was commonplace. There were so many fundamental differences between our kinds, it was no wonder we had lived so separately for so long.

"Adelina and Zane have a complicated relationship. She has been very vocal with her protests of this arrangement," Charis explained.

As if on cue, Adelina's voice rose outside the door. The words were not understandable through the heavy oak, but the tone was, and it suggested that Charis's assumption that there would be violence was not far off the mark.

The voices drifted down to silence, moving away through the hall. When it was quiet once more, Irene spoke.

"The ceremony will occur in the synkal— that's where any public event takes place and every serpiente is admitted. Zane is very popular among his people, which means the synkal will be full. You will be separated from the crowd for the actual announcement, but later you will be expected to move among them. The serpiente do not expect nor want distant monarchs; if you refuse to see your people, they will not tolerate you. No weapons are allowed in the synkal, and in addition to Zane, you will have a guard with you at all times. That should keep any surprised zealots from putting a knife in you this evening."

My blood had already turned to ice. I nodded calmly, past the point where I could be shaken. I was used to walking among my own people, but I *trusted* the ravens, crows and sparrows of my home.

"After that, the majority will be wary about starting fights. The guard will keep a lookout for troublemakers, but as I said, Zane is popular: If he seems happy, his people will follow him." Irene looked to Charis, as if wondering what she should say next.

Charis sighed lightly before asking, "Danica, how much do you know about our kind?"

The question took me aback. The answer was knowledge of how to fight them, and a hodge-podge of rumors and myths that might or might not be true. "Not much," I admitted.

"One thing my daughter would not think to mention," Charis continued, "is that there are some basic differences of behavior." At this Irene was listening as intently as I was. "In avian society—correct me if I am wrong, please—one is expected to behave with a level of distance and formality that is all but unknown among my people. As Tuuli Thea, you are expected to be more a symbol than a power, speaking with cool rhetoric and moving with simple grace. As Naga, the rules are different. A serpiente leader is a friend to her people and sometimes closer, occasionally a rival, but never detached. You've spoken with my son enough to know that every emotion he feels, he shows, and that is what is expected."

"Please go on," I said, trying to take in what she was telling me.

"Zane will not push you further than you are comfortable going," Charis assured me, "but the fact is that you are going to need to convince the serpiente that this is not a match of convenience. The Diente does not choose his mate for politics or money or whatever foolishness humans marry for. If the people think Zane chose you for any reason other than love, they will not accept you."

I tried to speak and found my throat too dry to do so.

"They will expect you to be afraid, but they will think you brave—especially since Zane plans to let it be known that you do not have the approval of your own kind yet, but are willing to go through with this and convince your people to agree with you later. He has turned this match into the very image of young, reckless love, and that is the image you will be expected to preserve among the serpiente public."

I nodded, not at all sure I would be able to follow through. As Zane had pointed out, I could not even meet his gaze without wanting to recoil. "And this will involve . . . ?"

"It will involve being closer than you are probably comfortable with," Charis stated bluntly. "Touching among my kind is not just common, it is expected. Stay near Zane; that you will need to do anyway. Forget your polite avian reserve. I'm not suggesting you two make love in the middle of the synkal floor, so you can cool that charming avian blush from your face, but you will have to touch him—even if it's just an arm around his waist. Remember, you are hopelessly in love. The two of you can't keep your hands off each other. Zane is determined not to overstep his bounds with you. He would risk the whole venture to keep from doing so. It will be up to you to take initiative and keep the masquerade going. Does that make sense?"

"I understand." Could one be cold as ice and still have her face on fire from such simply stated words? Apparently so.

Charis Cobriana nodded. She opened her mouth as if to say more, then closed it again. After a moment, she said, "Thank you, Danica . . . for being willing to do this. When Zane first suggested that we try to arrange a meeting with the Tuuli Thea and her heir, I was his loudest skeptic. When I heard the Mistari suggestion, I was horrified." She shook her head. "I would not have had the courage even to contemplate such an idea, much less the altruism to give up what you and Zane are giving up for your people."

Words tried to surface and failed. "Thank you" seemed too deferential, "You're welcome" too arrogant. Finally I settled with, "I have lost too many people to this war. There was no way I could refuse to go through with something that might keep others from the same end."

CHAPTER 11

I WAS GOING TO FAINT. I HAD NEVER FAINTED in my life; it was not a common avian dilemma. But at the moment, it was less terrifying than the thought of walking in front of a large group of serpiente when the only people present who might consider protecting me were Zane Cobriana and his personal guards—guards I trusted to defend me in a crowd as much as I would trust them to knife me at the earliest opportunity.

Finally I heard my cue and stepped from the antechamber and onto the dais at the north side of the synkal. Instantly I heard reaction from the crowd: shouts and questions, which were muted to dumb shock when I moved to Zane's side.

Zane's words were white noise in my ears as I stood beside him. I caught my hands trembling.

I remembered Charis's assurance that touching was common and even expected in serpiente society, and I wrapped an arm around his waist in an attempt to halt my own shaking. Zane seemed startled for a moment, then continued to speak, finishing with, "Allow me to introduce my Naga, Danica Shardae."

The palace guards were visible in the crowd; though they were not in uniform for the ceremony, I had been introduced to the majority of them by Irene that afternoon and assured multiple times that at least one of them would always be at my side. They had been prepared, and even though most of them had expressed doubts earlier, they did not allow that hesitation to show now as they knelt.

Like ripples in a pond, each guard who knelt was surrounded by other serpents who followed their lead. Within a few moments of the first guard's movement, all but four figures had recovered from their shock and knelt.

"Kendrick?" Zane's voice carried over the hall, an ounce of threat mixed with light inquiry.

"I don't know what..." Kendrick looked around himself and seemed to notice that he was one of very few who were making a spectacle of refusing Zane's chosen Naga. As he sputtered, one of the remaining four went down on his knee. "She's a hawk. . . ."

Zane appeared amused. "Really?"

"But, sir, she's Danica Shardae!" the poor man protested.

"I just said that," Zane responded, refusing to be ruffled.

"Zane." In contrast to his easily projected voice, mine was soft, intended only for Zane's ears. He turned to face me, ignoring for the moment the serpiente he had been in the process of turning into a fool. "You can't expect everyone to just accept this."

"Of course not," he responded softly, lowering his head so his lips were just a short distance above mine. He had wrapped his arms around my waist, and it suddenly occurred to me what our pair must look like to the court. "But I can expect everyone to pretend to."

Another of the four knelt while he was speaking. Kendrick and the woman who was still standing exchanged a glance across the room.

Zane brushed a kiss across my lips, so briefly that I had no time to respond, and then he straightened to speak to the court again. "Kendrick, there's no need for jealousy; you are welcome to go out and find your own beautiful hawk," Zane said lightly.

"Zane, this is crazy!" This came from the woman, upon whom Zane turned his gaze with a bit of a smile.

"Pamela, no doubt you are right. I must be stark raving mad." There was an amused murmuring in the crowd as Zane continued. "I must have lost my mind to want someone as beautiful and charming as this for my partner. To think Danica Shardae could possibly have walked into the synkal, despite protests from her guards and family, despite the fact that they might very well throw her out of the Keep for daring to answer my dearest prayer . . ." At that he went down on one knee before me, one of my hands clasped in his. ". . . for her to abandon all propriety and become my Naga."

By the end of the speech, Pamela was actually grinning. I could feel a similar expression on my own face at the dramatic humor with which Zane had spoken. The only thing that spoiled the moment was the glimpse I caught of white-blond hair as Adelina walked stiffly out the back of the synkal. My attention was drawn to Ailbhe, who looked after his sister for a moment, shook his head and returned his attention to the crowd.

"Zane—" Kendrick broke off as Zane tugged on my hand, bringing me down to kneel with him on the dais.

"May I?" Zane's voice was soft, as he reached forward and brushed a thumb across my lips.

I nodded.

In one graceful movement, Zane wrapped an arm around my waist and pulled me toward him, then gently pressed his lips to mine.

For a few heartbeats, I managed to ignore the fact that there were probably three to five hundred pairs of eyes on us.

I pulled back first, and Zane let me go with obvious reluctance; he kept an arm around my waist as we stood side by side, and with a sweep of his free hand he introduced simply, "Naga Danica Shardae, your people."

Two of the guard moved forward to flank us as we stepped down from the dais. Musicians took our place, and we were instantly surrounded by Zane's people . . . *my* people.

I hugged closer to Zane, feeling the flutter of my heart beating so fast it was a constant hum in my ears.

Serpents *moved* differently than I was used to, and put less space between themselves and others. The colors that surrounded me were equally foreign. Used to the warm brown or gold eyes of the avian court, here I was faced by hot garnet, sapphire and emerald gazes—jeweled tones as varied and exotic as the sensual outfits and the unreserved voices and expressions the serpiente wore. I was like a child raised without color who had suddenly been thrown onto a giant painter's palette.

It was impossible not to notice the warmth with which the serpiente greeted their Diente, or the chill with which many of them regarded me. Women found every excuse they could to reach out and put a hand on Zane's shoulder or arm.

Occasionally a man would attempt to be equally familiar with me. At that point, Zane would meet the serpent's gaze with a polite smile and a spark of ice in his eye and coolly remind the man that I had been raised an avian lady and was not used to casual touch from strangers.

In general, Zane handled the crowd like a magician, shifting from whimsy to melodrama to soft threat and back to whimsy as effortlessly as water flowing down a slope. It was eerie to watch the changes come over his face and body as he moved from one emotion to the next.

A few hours later the throng started to thin out, and a midnight feast was served for those who remained—about half of the people who had attended the ceremony.

"Zane, where is Adelina?" one female serpent asked as we settled into our places around the table. "It's rare to see you without her."

Zane's light expression clouded for an instant, but he recovered quickly. "The rest of the guard is quite competent. She wasn't feeling well, and since I wasn't expecting trouble tonight, I suggested she take the night off and let Ailbhe take over for a few hours." After having watched the play of emotion on his face all night, I knew he was lying.

But the serpiente nodded, not challenging Zane's words.

"Is Ailbhe going to lead Danica's guard?" another man asked.

Zane appeared surprised. "Adelina and Ailbhe will continue to lead the palace guard together," he answered. "Danica will, of course, be guarded by the Royal Flight."

The serpent choked on the wine he had been drinking, coughing and finally sputtering, "What?"

Others at the table seemed equally shocked. "You can't allow them into the palace," one woman shouted.

Zane met the woman's eye squarely, not threatening yet but bluntly honest as he asserted, "I certainly *can*, and I certainly *will*. Danica is my Naga, and you would do well to remember that she is yours, as well. I expect no one will attempt to challenge the presence of their queen's guards."

"With all respect, Zane," the man responded, "I can't see myself tolerating a flock of birds in—"

This time when Zane rounded his gaze on the speaker, his expression was strong enough that the man bit back the end of his comment. Quietly, Zane pointed out, "If you cannot tolerate it, then you are within your rights to attempt to deal with what you find to be a . . . distasteful infestation." I felt my cheeks color and was about to protest when Zane continued, his voice as cold as steel. "In that case, I would be well within *my* rights to charge you with treason, and both my guard and my Naga's will doubtless support the full punishment for that crime."

The man's face had gone white. "I didn't mean to imply that . . . Of course I wouldn't . . ." He looked around as if for backup, but found none. At last he gathered himself and finished, "If you believe they can be trusted in the palace, then it is not my place to contradict."

"Correct," Zane answered. "Now, shall we eat?"

The meal was good; the dishes had been carefully arranged so I was able to avoid meat without the other guests feeling deprived. Fresh bread, fruits, cheeses and elaborate vegetarian dishes were in abundance. Venison, rabbit, pork and beef made up the meat dishes; apparently Zane had decided poultry would be inappropriate.

It was nearly sunrise when Zane led me back to a room in which I would be able to stay. We had mutually decided that going home now would be both tactless—it would appear too impersonal to leave so shortly after the ceremony—and dangerous in my present condition. I was so exhausted, drained both physically and emotionally, that I had to lean against Zane to keep from weaving in the halls as we walked. I had left the Keep early, and now it was nearly sunrise again.

Laid out on the bed was a simple linen shift to sleep in, and I was relieved that someone had realized I would not be comfortable with the usual serpiente practice of sleeping in only one's skin.

"This room is part of my private suite," Zane explained, "and thus, it is one of the most protected areas in the palace. That should keep any disgruntled vipers from breaking in during the night. My room is through that door, the bathing room there and upon any future visits you may store clothing or other possessions in the trunks behind you. I took the liberty of having a few simple outfits made up, since it seemed likely an event like tonight's would occur and you would need something to wear." He paused, as if there was more he wanted to say.

When it became evident that he was not going to speak whatever else was on his mind, I allowed my curiosity to push me into asking, "How in the world did you get my measurements to have clothing made?"

Zane flashed a disturbing smile. "From Eleanor, of course."

Eleanor . . . "Eleanor Lyssia?" My voice was breathy with shock.

"Is that so surprising?"

Considering how easily she had agreed to

help me that night, it should not have startled me to learn that the seamstress had been working with Zane. I remembered her greeting me in the market and remarking on how I had comforted Gregory, and the unease I had felt when Zane revealed knowledge of those hours. When we were children, she had been so prone to mad schemes and so full of impossible dreams that it had shocked everyone when she had tamely decided to be a seamstress.

Another piece of information clicked suddenly into place. "You helped design this?" I asked, gesturing to the dress I was still wearing, which had been so perfect that I had never paused to question it.

"I suggested that you should be provided with something appropriate for tonight, yes," Zane acknowledged. "Though to give the credit where it is deserved, Eleanor outdid herself." The look in his eyes as they lingered on my form said more than his words and was enough for me to want to change the subject.

Zane seemed to notice my discomfort, for he cleared his throat and said more practically, "Eleanor did mention that the dress is difficult for one person to manage. Do you need help with it?"

Having Zane's assistance was quite different than having a maid or Eleanor help. However, as

I saw no other choice but to make a fool of myself trying to do it alone, I answered, "If you could undo the tie at the back of my neck, I can get the rest."

I turned around and tried not to jump at the feel of his cool fingers on the back of my neck. I lifted my hair away and felt him hesitate at the sight of my golden feathers before loosening the tie.

Awkwardly, I managed to pull the night shift over myself before dropping the burgundy dress, very conscious of Zane's presence.

As I carefully folded Eleanor's masterpiece to store it safely in the trunk, I heard Zane sigh.

"Danica—" He broke off as I turned to face him, and took a slow breath. "May I join you tonight?" My nervous expression made him continue quickly, "I'm not asking for anything beyond your company in *sleep*. Just let me rest with the sound of your heartbeat beside mine."

The request was spoken with something like wistful innocence, and I did not have the energy to be cruel enough to refuse. After Charis's statements earlier, and my observations in the synkal, it was not surprising that the new king of the serpiente would think it natural to sleep beside his Naga, even in a scenario as strange as ours.

The serpiente bed was designed with luxury in mind, piled high with blankets of the softest, thickest wool. As I lay on my stomach, the blankets and mattress sank beneath my weight until I was enveloped in a plush nest so comfortable that I felt sleep pulling at me instantly.

Zane stretched out on his side, still wearing slacks but having discarded his formal shirt. I was suddenly very aware of his arm across the back of my waist; he must have felt me tense, because while I bit back a protest, he was already moving to put more distance between us.

A sense of awkwardness hung between us for a moment, but exhaustion was a stern master, and it was not long before I was relegated to dreams.

CHAPTER 12

I N MY DREAMS, VASILI VOICED HIS APPROVAL of my choice, echoing Charis's words about altruism and adding to them words about courage. I took heart from his assurances, even though I knew they were only in my imagination.

When Rei appeared, furious, I listened to him rage over my decision and waited anxiously for the scene to change.

I dreamed last that I was at my own funeral. The avian court was in mourning, and as much as I tried, I could not get their attention.

WHEN I OPENED my eyes, it took me a few moments to realize that I was awake.

During my restless dreams I must have moved, and now I found myself lying on my back.

This change in position was not unusual for me. What *was* unusual was Zane resting against me, his body molded to the shape of mine. One arm was under my head, providing a soft, living pillow; the other was across my waist.

The position was so startlingly unexpected that I hardly knew how to react. I started to pull away, and then stopped as Zane turned closer to me in his sleep.

Again I shifted, and again he compensated, nuzzling against my hair, breathing in a gentle sigh. His arm tightened around my waist, hugging me close.

Asleep, Zane was not thinking about who he was lying next to, but I did not have the courage to wait and see what would happen when he woke. Trying not to disturb him, I slipped out of his arms, placing bare feet on the floor and shivering at the sudden chill.

I glanced back to see his eyes open, watching me.

"Morning," he said, voice soft. He stood and stretched, and suddenly I found myself a little too aware not just of his hypnotic garnet eyes, but of the broad shoulders and very bare chest that accompanied them.

I felt heat creep up my face and turned away, making a great pretense of searching through the trunk for a new outfit when there weren't really enough choices to make it difficult.

Zane knelt beside me. He touched my cheek gently, and for the first time his skin felt as warm as mine, as warm as his voice when he said, "Should I be flattered by that charming blush?"

Compose yourself, Danica. I took a deep breath, recovering the fringes of my control and poise until I could look back at him placidly. Before I could speak, Zane tensed, withdrawing his hand.

"Please don't," he said.

"Don't what?"

He stood up, putting distance between us as if I had suddenly sprouted claws. "I slept all night beside you, Danica. Please don't hide from me now."

"I don't know what you're talking about."

He sighed, shaking his head. "You breathe and move and speak, but whereas I would know a serpent was behind me even if he stood as still as a statue, when I stand in front of you now it is like I am looking at a picture, something flat. Sound and sight say you are there, but there is another sense that feels *nothing,* a sense that is completely blind."

He paused, as if searching for words to explain. Tentatively, I offered, "You can sense ... emotion." *And sense a void when I hide that emotion.*

He hesitated, as if turning the words over in his mind. "Serpiente legend, Danica ... says that your kind have no souls." I was about to argue, but he continued swiftly. "I believed it, until I

139

spoke to you in the Keep. You weren't guarded then; you lost your temper with me, actually." I had thought I was asleep, but I did not say that aloud as he went on. "And for the first time, I wasn't looking at a shell; I was looking at a real person. I was looking, I think, at the compassionate woman who comforted a dying man and who would soon become a beloved queen. Your 'reserve' is like armor; it may be your strongest weapon against my people. Surrounded by such ghosts, a serpiente soldier is as off balance as any sparrow looking into Cobriana eyes. But we aren't at war anymore," he finished softly.

My heart gave a heavy thump as he stepped back toward me, as hesitantly as I had ever moved toward him. He lifted his gaze, and I forced myself to look into his garnet eyes, which right now were rife with unease and a plea for trust.

Trust. I didn't know if I had the courage for that.

He stepped closer then, and kissed me, chastely and gently.

A heavy knock, followed almost immediately by someone pushing open the door, caused both of us to jump.

Adelina recoiled at the sight of us, and with blatant disgust in her tone, said, "I'm sorry for the intrusion, but there is a bird demanding to see your Naga." She nodded in my direction, and when she met my gaze, her pale green eyes made me shudder. "Since I can't put a hand on him to detain him, it seemed best to get her quickly to avoid a nasty scene."

"Andreios?" I asked, trying to recover my composure and feeling torn because I knew that I was doing exactly what Zane had asked me not to. He pulled away from me, not looking my way as Adelina spoke.

She nodded. "He says he is the head of your guard," she answered. "I suggest you hurry, before he comes looking for you."

There was no chance to speak with Zane about what had just happened. I hurried into clean clothing while Zane dressed in the next room and Adelina waited in the hall. I tied back the chaos my hair had become, and within a minute I was presentable enough to speak to Rei.

Adelina escorted me to the reception hall, where Rei was pacing anxiously. I saw tension go out of his body in a rush when he saw me walking toward him uninjured.

"Danica, thank the sky," he greeted me. "Eleanor gave me your letter. What are you doing here? This—" He broke off abruptly, as if just realizing we had an audience. To Zane he said, "I would like to speak to my Tuuli Thea alone, if I may."

His voice was dangerous, and Zane heeded the audible warning. "Adelina." He nodded toward the door, and his guard turned stiffly and exited. "Danica, I will be across the hall when you are finished."

Once the room was cleared of everyone but Rei and me, he began again to speak. "What are you *doing* here, Danica? Trying to get yourself killed?"

"Trying to end this war," I replied instantly. "And don't you see that it's working? Adelina didn't let you in because she took a fancy to you. Do you think the leader of the Royal Flight could possibly have made it this deep into the serpiente palace if Zane wasn't trying so hard to make peace?"

"Danica—"

I interrupted him, knowing that I would need to convince him quickly or have him argue with me forever. "I knew the risks, and I was and still am willing to take them," I assured him. "The serpiente are sincere. I stood in front of their entire court, Rei, and no one tried to harm me." There was wonder in my voice. "For the first time, I walked among them safely. I spoke with them, without bearing threats. They are willing to follow Zane into peace."

Rei sighed. "But what of you, Danica?" He shook his head in frustration. "I know you will do what you must for your people, but what about *you*?" He paused to take a deep breath, and then continued intently. "The danger is not only from soldiers. You were raised a lady, and you were raised avian. Zane Cobriana ... he will not understand that. He will expect more from you than you are prepared to give, more than any avian alistair would ask so quickly." He caught my hand, nearly pleading. "Danica, there are reasons our two kinds do not get along. We are not meant to. The serpiente are quick to anger and quick to show it. Even among friends there is violence."

"Rei, I need your support," I pleaded, letting my own self-control slip to match the emotion in his voice. "I know the serpiente are not the same as our people. I am not foolish enough not to be frightened. But I am willing to risk my life if that will keep me from holding another child while he dies."

Rei nodded reluctantly, his brown eyes still warm with worry. "I know," he said finally. "I wish I could convince you, but ... I know. You would not be the woman I love if you were not prepared to suffer for your people. But Danica—" He broke off, shaking his head, and instead asked, "You intend to announce Zane as your alistair tomorrow, I assume?" I nodded, grateful for his acquiescence. "I would recommend bringing Zane into the Keep with as few people's knowledge as possible. I will make sure the Royal Flight won't cause trouble, and the court is too well mannered to cause a scene in front of its

Tuuli Thea. Aside from my soldiers, the most zealous of your people will be guarding the Keep, not watching the ceremony." He returned to pacing. "They won't like it, obviously. They won't trust Zane, no matter how mellow his troops have been lately. But if you present yourself the same way you have to me—determined to do anything for peace—they will follow you. I hope."

I accepted his reasoning gratefully. Even when agitated, Rei had always been a clear thinker.

"My flight might be the greatest danger toward your plan," Rei continued. "Many of them would rather go against your orders than allow a cobra near their Tuuli Thea."

"I'm trusting you to keep them in line."

Rei sighed. "You know your mother is not going to agree with you."

"My mother is not Tuuli Thea anymore." My voice was solid, and for that I was grateful.

He nodded. "She has moved into one of the suites on the fourth floor of the Keep, and the Tuuli Thea's apartment has been prepared for you. The Royal Flight is going to be hard-pressed to defend both you and her from Zane if I also need to assign a guard to protect Zane from them."

"Zane can stay in one of the side rooms in the Tuuli Thea's suite," I suggested, having thought this out earlier. Seeing the arrangements for me at the serpiente palace had made me pause to consider what might be done at the Hawk's Keep. "There's only one staircase from or to the seventh floor, so it will be easy for your flight to keep track of Zane's movements and make sure anyone likely to attempt assassination is kept away."

Rei nodded thoughtfully. "Unfortunately, that puts you in the quick of danger if Zane causes trouble or if anyone tries to harm him."

"If he wanted to kill me, he would have done it," I answered peevishly, my patience wearing thin. "There are a half dozen rooms in the Tuuli Thea's apartment, and to get from any of them to my room, someone grounded would need to pass through the central hallway. The Keep was designed so one man in that hall can guard the entire floor."

Grudgingly, Rei agreed. "There are four of my guard in the surrounding woods," he explained. "They can serve as an escort for Zane so our soldiers don't kill him on sight." Rei glanced at the doorway. "I'll need to send Erica ahead. She's a good fighter, but she's one of the ones I don't trust to keep her knife sheathed if she has a chance to put it in a cobra's back. I'll speak to her once I get to the Keep and make sure she won't get too hasty. The rest . . ." He trailed off. "You know this entire idea sickens me?" He said the words coolly, but the emotion in his eyes was anything but.

"I know."

"If this is your decision, I know you'll do it no matter what I say." He sighed. "If I fight you on it, it will only endanger you more. I'm helping with this madness for that reason alone: so in the future you'll trust me enough to let me know what you're doing." When I nodded, he admitted frankly, "I would like to put a knife in him myself, and if he makes the slightest threatening move anywhere in your direction, I will. With your permission or without, Danica. See to it that your . . . alistair knows that."

Rei paused, then added more softly, "Be careful, Danica."

Again I nodded, throat closed against any response I could make to this rare display of emotion. "We should get Zane now," I said instead. The words were harsh, but necessary. Rei looked like he was on the verge of carrying me out of the serpiente palace, without care of propriety or promises of peace.

He let out a slow breath, and then we went to get Zane.

REI SENT TWO of his flight—Erica and Karl—to accompany me from the serpiente palace on wing.

Adelina and Ailbhe had only deferred to Rei's statement that he could not allow two of the palace guard into the Hawk's Keep because

Zane had forced them to. We could probably conceal Zane, but sneaking anyone else inside was asking for trouble, and if the palace guard were noticed before the ceremony, it would cause a panic. They would travel on horseback with Zane, Rei and two others in the Royal Flight until reaching the base of the Keep.

It was afternoon by the time I returned home. A party traveling on the ground would not traverse the distance as quickly, and I did not expect Rei and Zane to appear until that evening at least. But as day fell to night, I could not help worrying.

I did believe that the serpiente were sincere, but believing them and trusting them were entirely different matters. If a scuffle ensued between Rei's people and Zane's, I did not know who would win.

Feeling vaguely ill with nerves, I sank into my bed after dinner.

It was too late to back out of this, but I could not yet force my mind to accept the arrangement I had agreed to and all it entailed.

I was startled from my reverie by a knock on the door to my room.

"Yes?"

Rei opened the door, his long hair windblown and cheeks flushed. "Everyone arrived safely. One of the maids is preparing a room for Zane in the northern set," he informed me.

"Your mother has been staying in her own rooms, so we haven't had any trouble keeping Zane out of her sight." He stepped inside and closed the door behind him. "Danica, you're pale as a dove."

I put a hand to my cheek and felt the chill of my skin. "I'm frightened."

Rei caught my hand and raised it to his lips. "I will keep you safe." The words were a promise. "Even if it means defending Zane Cobriana from my own people so you can end this war as your ancestors should have, I will protect you." He sighed. "Do you believe me?"

"I believe you," I answered. I knew my smile was tired.

"Good night, Danica."

"Good night," I bid him softly.

He left, though I knew he would not be going far. He would not leave anyone else to guard my doorway with a cobra so near.

I slept well.

CHAPTER 13

ANXIETY WOKE ME EARLY THE NEXT MORN-
ing. I bathed and dressed quickly before
meeting up with Zane in the hall outside my
room. Andreios was exchanging a few last words
with Zane, detailing the scripted ceremony associated with the naming of an alistair, which Zane
appeared fairly amused to hear about.

"Tell me, do the three-year-olds usually
honor these vows?" Zane asked glibly.

Rei kept his control, but the tone of his voice
when he responded was sharp enough to tell me
that the comment was not the first one Zane had
made. "Yes, the *decision* is usually made when an
alistair is that young, but he doesn't take the
vows until he is ready. Hopefully you're old
enough that they're clear to you," he added

between clenched teeth. "If they aren't, I'm sure—"

"Good morning, Andreios," I said loudly, drawing both men's attention to me before someone was hit. "Good morning, Zane." If the two men ever did come to blows, the fight would be serious—deadly so—and I doubted they would both walk away alive.

I glanced toward the other two guards who stood in the hall with us, and added quietly, "Karl, Erica, stand down."

Both radiated tension. Erica especially trailed Zane with her eyes as if taking a sight for a notched arrow.

Karl flashed what looked like a forced smile. "Relax, Erica. We can always say 'just kidding' and run for our lives."

One of the lightest of tone among the Royal Flight, Karl had apparently been assigned to this job today to keep my mood from bleakness. His humor and voice almost served to disguise how raptly his attention covered the area, and particularly the cobra.

Erica did not appreciate the humor. "No disrespect, milady," she said to me with harsh formality, "but I will relax only when I am shown proof that he"—she nodded in Zane's direction—"is harmless."

I glanced at Rei, silently questioning his decision. I trusted their loyalty to me, but worried

150

that they might not go out of their way to protect Zane if someone meant him harm. In fact, both struck me as a little overzealous.

He answered the unspoken question. "I trust these two to be loyal to you without fault, and they've sworn not to harm him. When there are others of our kind around who might be a threat to your alistair, I will assign other guards. When you are alone with a serpent, I won't put someone in the way that might hesitate to fight him."

Erica and Karl both looked flattered by their commander's recommendation and unflustered by the implication that they were less than fond of Zane. Since Rei himself had for a moment sounded regretful that he couldn't let them kill their charge, I found it difficult to fault them.

Instead I looked at Zane, who offered a brave smile and a shrug.

The serpent was certainly making an attempt to look harmless. He had abandoned his normal black attire in favor of calfskin pants so light they were nearly golden, and a loose shirt several shades darker. The brown tones made his garnet eyes appear less red, and his fair skin warmer.

However, clothing could not completely disguise the smooth tension of his movements, so subtly different than any avian, or completely dim the fire in his gaze. I was dreading introducing him to my people.

"Milady, it is time." Eleanor was slightly

breathless as she darted into the room, her cheeks flushed with excitement.

Zane offered his arm, at the same time delivering to me a sardonic smile. "This is going to be interesting."

There was some carefully controlled surprise among my people when I first descended the stairs with Zane instead of Rei, but no instant fury. It occurred to me that most of these people had never seen Zane before, and unless they caught sight of the signet ring he was wearing or met his Cobriana eyes—something he had assured me he could avoid—they were unlikely to recognize him.

But as I crossed the room to the slight stage in the back of the court, I could see the ripple of unease in those nearby. Instincts. Even a sleeping dormouse wakes up and knows when the cat is nearby; so it was among the court. Zane, for all his attempts to appear harmless, would never pass for avian.

They looked at Rei, and at me, and at the other members of the Royal Flight who were standing nearby, but since my guards and I were not visibly upset, they assumed their own discomfort was imagined. Only the sight of the blood rushing from my mother's face as she fainted set my heart racing. Gerard caught her, looking a little surprised and unsure of what to do with his charge. Luckily, she had been standing at the far back of the room, and only those nearest to her had noticed. I would deal with her later. Now it was time to step onto the platform.

"Tuuli Thea Danica Shardae," Rei greeted me. "You have chosen this man as your alistair, as your protector, of your own free will and without coercion."

"I have." My voice did not tremble.

Rei turned to Zane. "Are you willing to swear upon your own spirit and the sky above that you will protect Danica Shardae from all harm?"

"Upon my own spirit, I will so swear."

"And do you swear you will never raise voice or hand against her?" Rei spoke the words calmly, but the expression in his eyes as he met Zane's gaze fearlessly was anything but calm.

Zane hesitated a fraction of a second; whether surprised by Rei's bold action or debating whether he was willing to so swear, I did not care to know. "Never would I willingly harm the woman I love."

Rei caught the wording, and for a moment I saw his jaw clench against the desire to argue. He knew as well as I that Zane had made no claims of love toward me, and that his promise not to harm the woman he loved did not protect me.

Rei's gaze flickered to me, beseeching, and I gave a nod for him to continue. I understood Zane's hesitation, despite how unnerving it was;

if it came down to a choice of him or me, he would defend himself and his people. He could not swear never to harm me without knowing whether peace between our two peoples would work.

"Danica Shardae is Tuuli Thea, and so when you swear to her, you swear to all her people," Rei continued, his voice sounding strained. "Will you protect the Tuuli Thea's people as you would your own family, and risk all that is necessary to defend them?"

"I swear upon the tears of the goddess Anhamirak, I will do everything within my power to stop the bloodshed among the Tuuli Thea's people." In those words I heard sincerity at last, and though I did not know the name of the goddess to whom Zane had made the vow, I knew from his tone that he was honest in his words.

There were scholars better educated than I among the court, and as I heard their frantic whispers, I knew that some had understood the reference. I also saw with dread that my mother was stirring. As Rei continued, I watched her set her feet on the ground, her reserve shattered and her face holding abject horror.

"Danica Shardae, Tuuli Thea, you have chosen this man as your alistair," Rei continued formally, his voice rising slightly above the noise in the crowd. "Zane Cobriana, you have sworn to defend Danica Shardae, your Tuuli Thea. Upon the words you have spoken, you are bound for life."

Those words *for life* had a fateful ring.

A hush descended over the avian court, and in those moments, as I waited for a reaction, I met my mother's gaze. She looked at me with sadness and anger and shook her head. Then she began to walk out the back of the room.

Gerard tried to stop her, and I saw her spine go rigid. "The Tuuli Thea has made her choice. My words are meaningless here," she said loudly without turning. I nodded to the guard, and he hurried after the Tuuli Thea he had first served as she left.

Her rejection cut, but I had expected it.

With a deep breath to loosen the knot in my throat, I stepped forward. The court quieted, awaiting my words, stunned by what they could not believe.

I stated simply, "Yes, it is true. This is Zane Cobriana you see before you." I had to raise my voice slightly over the protests as I continued. "Yes, it is Zane Cobriana who has just sworn to defend your Tuuli Thea—and you." That quieted them slightly, and I took advantage of the silence. "When the serpiente first spoke to me of peace, I was doubtful. But I am your queen, and as such, I am willing to do what I must to protect you, my people. That means ending this war any way I can."

I stood at attention, left hand grasping my right wrist behind my back—the pose of a soldier, which I had picked up from Rei and Vasili when I had been a girl. I knew everyone who had ever fought in our armies or lost someone from our armies would recognize the posture.

"You know me," I implored them. "You know that I do not avoid going out to the field and caring for the wounded. You know that I do not flinch from the bodies that must be brought home. I do not intend to be a queen who ignores the suffering of her people. I have held your own children's hands, and talked to them as they died, so they would not be alone. And I am tired of it."

I took Zane's hand, grasping it on the stage in the avian court, in front of so many avian ladies and gentlemen who were shocked by even that small contact.

"I feared this man, as you do. I hated him, as you do. But when our soldiers cut down his brother in the field, I was the one left to sit by that boy's side as he died. And he was no different than my brother who died the same day, or the alistair and family I lost when I was a child. Then Zane came to me, asking for peace, and I had to listen." I took a breath, trying to calm myself. I had not meant to get so carried away, but now the court was watching me in amazement. Perhaps that was a good thing. "Zane has sworn to defend my people, and as Naga of the serpiente I am equally sworn to defend his."

There was some more protest at this last statement, and I waited for it to die down before I said softly, "We have all lost loved ones. And if I need to go onto the field and disarm every frightened soldier by hand, alone in the night, I will do it. As of this moment, I declare this war over. Any injury done to the serpiente will be looked upon as injury to *my* people, and to *your* people."

The court did not know how to react. They had been raised avian and were not taught to loudly express outrage or fear. However, under the circumstances, polite caution and distaste could not cover what they wanted to say.

Finally, one soft voice pervaded the area. "Milady, how can we be sure of their intentions?" The crowd parted so the woman who was speaking could approach me. "Of course I have faith in you and your judgment, but might the serpiente even now be planning to attack as soon as you recall our soldiers?"

"I had a similar thought when Irene Cobriana first came to the Keep to ask for a meeting in Mistari land," I admitted. "The Royal Flight and my own family both cautioned me against trusting the serpiente, and I was spirited back to the Keep. But Zane was not that easily dismissed," I recalled. "And when he showed up in my suite a few weeks later, unbeknownst to my guards, my mother and everyone else in the Keep, it was hard to believe that he intended me harm."

Rei was visibly perturbed by these words, but he said nothing as I continued to speak. "Had the serpiente wanted to injure me, there would have been opportunity—here in the Keep, and at the serpiente palace on the two occasions that I have visited there. Yet I stand before you unscratched." I spoke softly, but I knew my voice would carry in the near-silence of the court. "I ask for trust. I ask that I might never again hold another dying soldier—avian or serpiente—in my arms. I ask for trust. I ask that you put away your weapons so we can mourn the dead properly, and then move on. I ask for trust. I ask that your children can learn of peace instead of war. I ask for trust. It is a lot, I know; it isn't easy to give. But it is *all I ask*."

CHAPTER 14

Escorted by Andreios and Karl, Zane and I withdrew, leaving the court alone to make their decisions. I heard several voices raised, among them Eleanor, loudly declaring their support before anyone else could speak.

After Zane and I had settled onto the balcony that marked the highest point in the Keep, I asked, "Who is Anhamirak?" Two of the Royal Flight were waiting discreetly on the stairs down to the main apartment; Rei had reluctantly gone to bed after what must have been more than a full night and day awake.

"Hmm?" Zane's gaze was distracted as he looked out over the surrounding forest and distant mountains and doubtless wondered how the argument back in the court was going. If it went

159

badly, there were seven floors between him and safety.

"Anhamirak," I repeated, trying to keep either of us from mulling over what was happening. "You swore to her during the ceremony, when Rei asked whether you would defend my people as your own."

"When Egypt was young, and the first pyramids were being built with the sweat and blood of slavery," Zane recited, not turning his gaze from the view, "there was a sect of thirteen men and women, the high priestess of whom was a woman called Maeve. They worshiped a goddess named Anhamirak, who ruled over life, light, love, beauty—and above all, free will."

Zane sighed. "As the myth goes, a creature by the name of Leben appeared to Maeve and instructed her to stop her worship of Anhamirak and turn it onto him. He was powerful, but not a god, and Maeve knew it. She seduced him, and in an attempt to gain her favor, he gave to her ageless beauty and the second form of an elegant viper with ivory scales. She demanded that he do the same for all her people, including a woman named Kiesha. To Kiesha, Leben gave the form of a king cobra, and from her son—or so the story goes—the Cobriana line is descended."

"Do you believe it?" I asked, rather entranced by the tale.

"I believe this." Zane held up a hand, and I

could not help stepping back as the ink-dark snakeskin rippled into appearance over his bare skin, only to subside again as if it had never existed. "And I believe this." I had been watching him so intently that I had no chance to avert my gaze as he lifted garnet cobra's eyes, halting the air in my lungs. "I have seen the serpents dance, and if it isn't magic, I can find no better word." He looked away, returning those frightening jeweled eyes to the landscape as he leaned against the balcony railing. My breath let out in a rush. "What about you, Danica?" he asked. "What do you believe in?"

The story behind my kind was equally magical, but it had always been told to me as just that: a story and nothing more. Now I moved beside Zane and looked out at the land that held his attention. "I believe in the air beneath my wings when I soar."

"Is this what the world looks like when you are flying?"

I tried to see the land below as would someone who had not seen it from this height every day. The sky was just beginning to color with the pink and violet streaks of twilight, and long shadows streaked the ground. "It's not as clear as this," I responded, trying to recall what the ground *did* look like to a hawk in flight. "When you fly, the air is mostly what you are aware of . . . how it moves, and how you move in it. The ground isn't important unless you are diving, landing or falling."

"Falling?"

I had been hit once by a serpiente arrow, clipped in the wing while I was flying from a battle. Falling, unable to steady myself for several seconds, I had only escaped the deadly impact with the ground because one of Rei's soldiers had caught me. It was not a moment I wanted to dwell on—or repeat.

"It happens sometimes" was all I told Zane.

"Milady?" The voice came from a very hesitant young sparrow, whose gaze flickered to and from Zane with bright fear. "When you have a moment, your mother would like to speak to you and your . . . alistair." She hesitated, as if my mother had used different words to describe Zane.

"She is welcome to come speak to me at any time," I responded, both relieved that my mother was unlocking herself from her room and dreading the confrontation to come. "Kindly invite her to join us here."

The sparrow bobbed a clumsy curtsy and disappeared quickly.

"I think she's afraid of me," Zane observed, a dark humor showing through in his tone. He leaned back against the railing, crossing his arms, then pausing—like a cobra, coiled and waiting, a deep stillness seeping into him as he prepared to face my mother. I wondered if he even realized how dangerous he appeared in that moment.

My kind lets off subtle signs of life even when we're not moving: the heat of our bodies and the quick pace of our heartbeat. When Zane stood still, even his breathing slowed, as if he might simply dissolve into the night. The only sign of life in him was the flash of light off his iridescent gemstone eyes.

Please don't hide.

I wondered if, when I looked at him now, I saw and felt what he did when I pulled on my mask of avian reserve. If it was true . . . I could see how the myths had begun, saying we had no souls.

The time had passed for me to respond to Zane's forcedly light remark, and now an awkward silence stretched between us, both of us hidden behind our own shields and both unnerved by them.

"I think she's not the only one," he added under his breath as my mother ascended the stairway.

"Danica Shardae, you are Tuuli Thea now, and I have no power to override your decisions." Nacola's voice was forced, as if she had rehearsed this speech many times before coming to me. "But I will not support your agreeing to this sickening arrangement."

"I'm sorry to hear that." I truly was. My

mother's approval was something I had always strived for, and the lack of it now left me groundless. "But my people must come before even you, Mother. As your people should come before your daughter."

"Child, I would not protest so if I thought this would work," my mother argued. "I understand the sacrifices a queen must make for her people. But those sacrifices must be for a reason, and *this* . . . this is a reasonless act. Our two kinds are not meant to live together, Danica," she said softly. "From the very first we have been enemies, and so it will be until either they are destroyed or we are."

"You're absolutely correct." I jumped at Zane's voice, and my gaze shifted to him. "Snakes and birds are not creatures intended to live together. As I recall, hawks will snatch young cobras from the nest and eat them. But surely you are forgetting something rather important, milady Nacola." He paused there and waited as if for an answer.

My mother did not reply, and finally Zane just sighed.

"The first of my kind was a human woman. Surely your kind comes from like roots. We have human minds and human bodies. If we can speak as humans do, and love as humans do, then what makes us so different?" Zane's words were simple, but the anger and hope behind them were anything but. "Serpents and birds are not meant to live together," he asserted again, "but I personally like to believe that we are more than our animal counterparts."

"Your *people*," my mother spat, in a rare show of fury, "murdered my *parents*. My sisters, my husband, my son and my daughter—"

"And your *people*," Zane replied with equal vehemence, "have taken from me a father, two uncles, three brothers, a sister and a niece who had not even drawn her first breath. What possible harm had that infant done to you?"

He turned away as if he did not trust himself to face her, and he paced to the railing.

"Milady Nacola," he said tightly, "I don't want to fight with you. I fear I lose my temper too easily for your world's standards. What I am trying to say is that *I* am willing to forgive history and try to act as the human blood in me implores."

"Your temper is renowned," my mother responded, her voice once again under control, and acid in its detachment. "Your kind has never been famous for holding in check its tongue or its hands, and I wouldn't expect its king to do any better." Zane drew a breath as if to speak, but my mother continued. "With that in mind, surely you can understand my reluctance to trust you with my daughter."

"I have given my word I will not harm her,"

Zane interjected, but my mother simply shook her head.

"And when that Cobriana temper breaks loose, what then?" she argued, for all intents and purposes ignoring my presence. "Violence is common among the serpent court, or so I hear, and accepted to a much greater degree than it is in the Keep. I don't expect Danica has had much experience with being struck, and I don't wish her to gather such familiarity."

"Nacola—"

"Allow me to finish." To my shock, my mother met Zane's eyes with her own fiery golden gaze, and Zane was the one who looked away. "If I am to have no say in this decision, I would at least speak my mind to you."

"Continue." The word was tense, and Zane pointedly avoided looking at me as he said it.

My mother stepped closer. "If you ever put a hand on my daughter—"

"I assure you, fair Nacola, I've no intent to bruise such soft skin as Danica's. With that point overemphasized, is there anything else you would like to accuse me of?"

"She is not one of the casual women of your court, Zane," my mother argued next.

"Quite obviously," came Zane's silken reply.

"Your word that you will never force her to your bed."

The order came difficultly to my mother's

lips, and Zane recoiled in response, his eyes narrowing in fury.

"Would my word mean anything to you, Nacola? The word of a cobra, for your daughter's *virtue*?"

My mother hesitated, her lips parting as if she would speak and then sealing closed again without a sound passing them. Her gaze was hard, clearly speaking the answer: No, his word would mean nothing to her.

"Leave now, Nacola Shardae." Zane's voice was cold as ice.

"I—"

Zane whirled to face me, turning from my mother's protest. "Danica, get her out of here before I hurt her."

I stumbled back, but did not stop to question him. I caught my mother's arm, imploring her, "Mother, please return to your room now."

"Danica—" She broke off, and with one more fleeting look at Zane, she nodded.

We walked in silence until we reached the doorway to her room, the place where my sister had once slept, long ago when I had been a child.

"I know you will go through with this," my mother said flatly, her voice soft and sad. "Even Karashan admits that you are too brave for any of us to change your mind, Danica. But please don't let that courage make you careless. Keep a guard within shouting range, and never let the door lock when the two of you are alone. Sleep with a knife under your pillow if you must, and be careful, because he *will* hurt you if you do not protect yourself." She sighed, her voice a whisper as she added, "History repeats itself too easily."

I thought of the knife in the back that had ended Alasdair's life and nodded. The events of both this evening and the past forced me to respect my mother's words.

I returned to my balcony to find Zane gone; the guards informed me that he had retreated to his room and asked not to be disturbed until next dawn by anyone but me.

CHAPTER 15

TENTATIVELY I KNOCKED ON ZANE'S DOOR. I do not know what mad instinct possessed me to do so, but I did not think it wise to let the night pass without speaking to him.

I implored Karl, the guard assigned to this hallway, to stand outside the room instead of following me in. I did not know what kind of mood I would find Zane in, and worried that my guard might act too hastily.

"Enter." Zane's voice was husky, as if he had been shouting, though I had heard nothing.

I pushed open the door to the double rooms that Zane had made his own. The curtains to the circular balcony were normally open in good weather, but tonight they were drawn closed; only faint streaks of twilight seeped through the woolen window covering, and it took me a few seconds to adjust my eyes to the dimness.

Zane was sprawled across the low couch in the front room, his gaze resting contemplatively upon the bands of light that fell under the window.

He raised his eyes to me when I stepped into the room, but made no move to stand.

"Questions, Danica?" His voice was light, almost musical, betraying no hint of his earlier anger. Only the scant light reflected in his eyes still showed that violent emotion. "Do you want to ask, or would you prefer not to know what you have tied yourself to?" The spark of his eyes and the singsong quality of his voice made the feathers on the back of my neck rise.

"Are there questions I should ask?"

Now Zane stood, the act as liquid and threatening as his serpent counterpart coiling to strike, and I jumped at the movement. I saw the vague amusement on his face as he noticed my reaction.

"Relax. I'm not going to bite," he said, but of course the words were not intended to relax me.

Every instinct screamed at me to run, that there was a predator in the room, but I could not have moved a muscle if I had tried.

As Zane approached, he moved with a slow beauty and deadly silence. "So easy, Danica," he whispered, and now the pain was back in his voice and in the eyes that held me frozen where I stood. "Despite how I have despised your kind for so many years...you alone are so very fragile."

He lifted his hand, and I saw it coming but could barely move. At last, too late to turn away, I managed to break his gaze and close my eyes as I prepared for him to hit me.

He checked the blow so close that I felt the air ruffle my hair, but when he touched my skin, it was not in anger; all I felt was a soft caress, the backs of his fingers brushing over my cheek.

"So easy, Danica. If I had wanted to hurt you, I would have."

I pulled away, my breath coming quickly as Zane continued.

"I can feel the beating of your heart, Danica. And I know that if I pressed my lips to your skin right now, I would taste its sweet flavor, and smell the exotic scent that makes me want to bury my face in that damnably golden hawk's hair."

I hit the wall with my back and braced myself there.

"But as much as I want you, there is one emotion alone that can overcome lust, and that is fear." His voice as he said this was almost inaudible, it was so soft. "Never, Danica, will I touch a woman who fears me. Never will I strike or otherwise harm you unless you precipitate that violence by intending injury toward me or those I love. If we are in understanding on that, then you may be assured that this serpent is no threat to you."

I had no words with which I could respond.

Finally, Zane turned his back on me. "It's late, Danica, and tomorrow will doubtlessly be a long day. Now would be the time to return to your own bed . . . unless, of course, you plan to share mine."

Even if he looked as innocent as he had the last night I had shared his bed, after the ravages of anger, threat and insinuation that had passed his lips this night . . . I couldn't imagine being bold enough to join him.

But now, as he paused in the doorway, glancing back with an expression that danced between amusement and dismissal, a flicker of anger slid over my fear. Before I thought better, I stepped forward to meet his challenge.

"Okay." I knew my tone was not friendly.

Zane tensed, his eyes widening for a swift moment. "Excuse me?"

"You are my alistair," I responded. My voice was calmer than my thoughts. "It is considered impolite to make a spectacle of it, but it is not scandalous for a lady to stay a night with the man she is tied to."

I was just in front of him now. Zane was

watching me with a shocked fascination that gave me the courage to continue.

"What *would* be considered inappropriate is venting your anger at my mother's words on me." Zane jumped when I raised my gaze to his. I knew he could hold me if he tried, but he did not, and that made me bolder. "You've succeeded in frightening me, if that was your goal."

At these words, I saw him sag. Quietly, he answered, "I did not intend to frighten you."

I let my expression ask the question.

When he spoke again, his voice was careful. "Your mother all but accused me of something that is, among my kind, the highest crime a man can commit. There is no trial, only punishment, because it is considered better to let an innocent man die than let a guilty one live." He took a heavy breath and let it out. "I know my kind has an evil reputation in the eyes of yours, but having that ignorance thrown in my face in such a way was more than unpleasant."

I waited for him to continue, forcing him to fill the silence.

"I apologize for my temper, and for being too furious to argue sanely with your mother. Among my kind, the constant control avians exercise over their emotions would be considered . . . beyond rude, a lie to those around you. So I am not in the habit of needing to conceal my emotions, even where such control is a necessity. Even so, I apologize for frightening you when you did nothing to deserve my anger."

"You are forgiven, by me at least." I was still trying to push back the rioting emotions of the last few moments, but my heartbeat had almost returned to normal. "My mother will not be so quick."

Zane shrugged, and the movement betrayed his fatigue as his words had not. "Your mother is neither my mate nor my queen." His hands on my waist were so gentle I barely noticed the touch as he drew me forward. He kissed me lightly, just the barest contact. "You, milady, are both." He released me and smiled tiredly. "We both need sleep, Danica, something you would not find in my bed tonight."

I looked away at the implication in his words. "Good night, Zane," I replied.

"Good night, Danica Shardae." He sighed, and I heard the door to the adjoining room, which Zane had set up as his bedroom, close even before I had exited the front parlor.

"Everything all right, milady?" Karl asked worriedly as I stepped through the door into the hall.

"Fine," I responded.

"You look a bit shaken," he observed.

"A bit," I admitted. "But I will be fine. Thank you."

"May I speak bluntly, milady?"

I nodded, forcing myself to gather my wits and stand before the guard as his monarch, not as a scatterbrained chick. "Go ahead."

"I understand this arrangement is very important to you." Karl spoke with slight hesitation, picking his words carefully. "I understand that some risks are necessary. But some of the Royal Flight are worried that you are endangering yourself more than the situation demands." He nodded toward the door to Zane's room, and I knew he had been upset by my leaving him in the hall while I spoke to the cobra alone. "That you might not be willing to call to us until it is too late, out of worry for the peace." He took a breath and continued. "The Royal Flight is sworn to defend you, but we cannot do that if you will not let us."

I did not know how to reassure him. I had Zane's word he would never harm me, but he had also admitted his temper. If that temper got the better of him someday, would I keep my silence, or tell my guards and let them tear our fragile peace apart?

"I will think on your words." I was certain that Karl's worried questions would reverberate through my dreams all evening. "For now, good night."

"Good night, Shardae," he bid me. I saw him glance at Zane's door as if he was considering confronting my new alistair, but he just shook his head.

I hesitated. "Your concerns about my alistair wouldn't persuade you to leave him unprotected?"

"My commander and my Tuuli Thea have assigned me to guard this door and the serpent inside. I have sworn my loyalty to you and would not renege that word now. I swear no harm will come to your alistair so long as he is within the walls I protect."

I wondered as I walked down the hall whether Zane rested uneasily within the Keep, surrounded by guards who would only defend him in spite of their hatred for him.

In my room, the curtains to the balcony were still open wide. The moon was barely a fine crescent, but the stars shone brightly.

When I was a girl, Vasili had joked with me that when I was strong enough, I could fly to the moon.

Such fairy tales had disappeared when he had died.

I had lost too many dreams to blood. If the price to end that bloodshed was dealing with Zane Cobriana . . .

I lay on my bed, hoping I would sleep and dream of Vasili, that I could speak to him of all the things I could not tell people in this world.

In the serpiente court, I had to pretend to be in love with someone I could not be alone with unless I could bear his shifting moods and sudden outbursts. In the avian court, I had to pretend to be sure and self-sacrificing, when in reality I was sure of very little.

Even the questions I wanted to ask about Zane and our decisions were denied to me, for who would I ask? In the past, my mother and Rei had been those I trusted to give me answers, but they were against this venture, and I did not want to show them the depth of my fear. I considered speaking to Eleanor, as she supported what I was doing, but that thought only led me to wonder how much of what I told her would get back to Zane.

I began to pace in my room, too agitated for sleep.

I walked out to the balcony, where another guard was waiting in case Zane tried to enter my room that way.

"Good evening, Shardae," Gerard greeted me formally.

"I'm going for a flight," I announced. The guard nodded, without asking if I would like company. I would have someone with me whether I wanted to or not. The Royal Flight was not in the practice of letting its Tuuli Thea go anywhere alone.

After the strain of the day, it was a blessed relief to shift into my hawk's form and spread my wings.

My path traveled nowhere in particular, though out of habit I avoided serpiente lands. I flew until the night was deep, just a few hours until dawn, allowing the steady beat of golden wings and the movement of the air around me to be my only thoughts.

CHAPTER 16

THE NEXT FEW DAYS WERE FILLED WITH desperate attempts to keep the peace. To their credit, the Royal Flight and Ravens reacted quickly when news came that there was an altercation occurring on the boundary of serpiente and avian land; by the time they arrived, the serpiente palace guard had almost brought the situation under control. The leaders of the two rebel factions had been killed in the fight, including Erica Silvermead's father. She asked to be dismissed from the Royal Flight for a period so she could see to the arrangements and mourn as was proper, and her request was granted.

Zane and I made plans to travel weekly between the palace and the Keep, flanked usually by three of the palace guard and three of the

Royal Flight. Andreios handpicked the guards, to ensure that they would be vigilant about my safety and wary of the serpiente, but not hasty to cause trouble. I hoped that Adelina had picked her people as carefully; the coldness with which she always addressed me did nothing to put me at ease.

As the days passed, Zane spoke little to me beyond what was necessary to preserve the charade we held in front of his people. We avoided being alone together, unwilling to face anything more than our mutual efforts toward peace.

At the Keep, things continued as usual. Petitions were made of the Tuuli Thea, but rarely now did I receive pleas for aid against Zane's people. When such requests were made, the reaction came from the serpiente army, who took care of their own people more efficiently than our soldiers ever could have.

I explored the serpiente palace whenever I had a moment free, despite Zane's warnings of "Keep a knife handy, Danica, or better yet, a guard. There are some dark passages that would easily make an end to you if someone wanted to attempt it." I followed his advice when I was in unknown areas, though I spent most of my time in the main hallways.

I located the storerooms, the kitchen, the infirmary, the guardroom and countless other rooms. One entire side of the palace was open to the public and contained a forum, much like our market, that opened into the outside air, a gaily colored nursery and magicians and artists aplenty. At first I traveled everywhere with Rei or one of his people, but as time passed, the Royal Flight trusted more and more the palace guard to keep me safe.

Especially when I was traveling with an avian soldier, I was too often greeted with fear, but occasionally the rare serpent would approach and speak to me. These people were not surprised to see their Naga among them, but many seemed impressed that I had dared to join them. The air was rich with laughter, heady scents of exotic perfumes and the heavy web that seemed to connect all these people.

One afternoon, I watched the serpents' dance, a hypnotic and sensual ritual. The music was provided by a pair of musicians, one of whom beat out the rhythm on a low drum he held in his lap, while the other swayed with a flute.

The dancer was a young woman with eyes as bright as polished emerald and midnight black hair that tumbled nearly to her knees in wild waves. When she moved, the silken garments she wore rippled, showing as much as they concealed.

When she ended the dance, she was offered food and drink by her fans, with whom she flirted for a while before approaching me.

"That was impressive." I searched for a stronger word, but could not find one.

The serpent smiled, a playful smile that reminded me of Zane's when he was in a light mood. "That was Maeve's dance, from the Namir-da," she explained. "I will perform here in the midsummer night, for those who cannot watch the dance in the synkal." She paused, taking a sip of the rich wine someone had offered to her, and then said reflectively, "Or perhaps I might dance in the synkal this year, since Zane cannot."

"Why not?" Though I had recognized the name of Maeve from Zane's description of serpiente origins, I knew not about this dance.

The dancer seemed surprised at my question. "Because a mated man does not dance Namir-da with another woman, and, little hawk, I don't think you know the steps." She sighed. "Zane is a beautiful dancer. He performed last year with Adelina, and I much regret that I did not watch." A slight puckering appeared between the woman's brows. "We were surprised when Zane chose you. He is not known to be fickle, and he and Adelina . . ." She shrugged.

The words were a blow. I had known from

the first that Adelina hated me, but I had been too much of a coward to consider why.

The dancer did not seem to notice my discomfort. With one last sip of wine, she kissed the drummer on the cheek and began to climb back onto her stage. She paused on her knees so our gazes were nearly level. "I do not know whether a hawk could learn the Namir-da, but if you are willing to learn, I will try to teach you. Maeve was light and golden like you are," she added.

"I don't have much talent for dance."

"Perhaps not, but when have you tried? Your people do not move as serpents do. Maybe that is because they can't," she admitted, "but I should like to teach you. Come back this evening, hawk-let." With those words she stood, raising her hands into the air with her palms clasped together as if she was imploring some ancient god or goddess. The drum began, and my would-be tutor closed her eyes for a moment, and then began to move to the rhythm.

I had a few hours to decide whether I would take the woman up on her invitation. I had watched her performance with envy and would have loved to replicate it, but I doubted I would ever be able to. Music was important to my people, but dance was far too raw a form of expression for it ever to be popular.

I did have one decision already made: I needed to speak to Adelina. I did not know what I would say, but I felt I should recognize her sacrifice.

I found my way to the guardroom without fault. At this time of day Adelina would probably be out, but I knew she was not on patrol, and someone might know where she was.

I knocked on her door, but received no response. The guardroom dining hall was nearly empty, and the two serpiente there knew only that Adelina had left a few minutes ago.

Another time.

Zane was attending to some routine chores, so for the moment, I had nothing pressing to do.

Perhaps the archery range would offer some amusement. Serpents, like my kind, were practiced archers. I was learning from Ailbhe how to use the serpiente-style bow, though I hoped I would never need to use the weapon as more than entertainment.

An avian archer struck primarily to deliver deadly poison in an otherwise small injury. While the wound caused was minimal, the poison could kill a serpent in a heartbeat, but do little more than cause fatigue in an avian soldier.

The serpiente bow was larger and had a stiffer draw, and the arrow was plain and smooth, designed to fly far and penetrate as deeply as possible. It shot an arrow hard and fast, so a good aim could take a bird from the sky. I had been warned more than once to be careful if I ever used the weapon to defend myself, as a serpiente arrow that did not meet with the resistance of bone could at a close distance pierce through the intended opponent and strike anyone who stood behind—friend or foe.

I halted abruptly at a turn in the hallway as I glimpsed a couple entangled in the shadows of the next corner. I started to turn away to leave the two in privacy, but my eye lit upon white-blond hair I could not help recognizing.

Adelina?

I turned back just in time to see Zane—for even in the darkness, I knew it was him—draw in a ragged breath and push her away.

I heard his voice, soft and torn. "Adelina, we can't be doing this."

"We *are*," she responded practically.

"You know what I mean." His voice was a little more solid now, but no happier. "Danica—"

"Danica can rot for all I care," Adelina said, snarling. She took a breath, and then said more calmly, "Zane, I'm sorry. But we both know you don't love her. You can pretend to the court, but not to me."

"Adelina . . ." He sighed. A moment passed, a murmured word from Adelina I could not understand, and then, "Adelina, I wish we could, but I *can't*."

"You think the hawk would care?" Adelina challenged.

"I don't know," Zane answered. "But she is my mate. I wish . . . but wishes don't stop wars."

I had eavesdropped enough; this was an interaction more personal than I had a right to hear. But Adelina's voice rose and followed me down the hall as I walked away.

"Zane, I watch you and you are miserable," Adelina cried. "You are beautiful and strong and you should never be lonely."

"Adelina—"

"No!" She was nearly shouting now. "You are a cobra, Zane. A descendent of Kiesha. You are not a creature intended to live without the comfort of touch, yet that is what you are trying to do now."

Finally she softened her voice so I could no longer hear her. My step was quick and my route wide as I stayed as far away from that solitary corner of the palace as I could. Adelina's words were gnawing at my gut.

I didn't want Zane miserable, if Adelina was right about that, but he was still a cobra, and I could not make myself forget the power he wielded. Besides, how could I take the place of the woman who loved him?

The head of the palace guard being so vocal about her feelings for me made me nervous, too. I had no doubt now that Adelina would never warm to me. I only hoped Zane's guards' loyalty to him would keep me as safe as my guards' loyalty kept him.

I ran into Zane's sister a few paces down the hall from her room. Irene was leaning back against the wall, breathing very slowly and carefully.

Though I saw no injury, I could not ignore the sight.

"Irene, are you all right?" My other worries momentarily shoved aside, I helped her into her room, where she sat carefully on the edge of the nearest chair.

"I'll be fine," she asserted. "Just a bit of a spell." At my look of confusion, she elaborated, "I get them sometimes, with the baby. Luckily, my mother makes a wonderful raspberry-ginger tea."

I faintly remembered Zane mentioning that Irene was with child, and that she had been white with fear when she had told him.

"Don't look so worried, Danica," Irene said lightly. "I just chased the father off for hovering. I don't need you doing the same."

"Who is the father?" My relief that he was still alive was palpable.

"Galen," Irene responded, her voice carrying a bit of a sigh. "He's one of the guard. He was with us at the Mistari camps."

Thinking back, I did recall the lightly built

man who had sat beside Irene among the Mistari, though I did not think I had ever heard him mentioned otherwise.

As if reading my mind, Irene told me, "We were trying to keep it quiet—so he would not be more of a target than he already was. If things are still calm by then, we are going to make the announcement at the Namir-da."

There was that word again. "One of the dancers in the market mentioned the Namir-da to me."

"That would be A'isha, most likely; she is the leader of the local dancer's nest." Irene observed, "She is very talented, isn't she?"

I needed to confide in someone, but I had not intended the words to sound as desperate as they did when I said, "She says Zane and Adelina danced last year?" Irene nodded, her gaze distant. "Is Zane really so miserable?"

Irene looked startled by the question. She paused a moment before answering carefully, "He is very happy that the Mistari suggestion seems to be working. But peace, as wonderful as it is . . . peace does not keep anyone warm at night." More sure in her words, she continued, "Serpiente children are never alone, Danica. If their parents cannot be with them, they stay in the nursery, surrounded by playmates even in sleep, comforted by the nearness of others.

"Maybe in nature a serpent is a solitary

creature, but I can tell you that my kind is not. That is why the idea of Zane's choosing a mate for politics and not for love was so disturbing. Because no one—not myself, not even Zane—believed an avian could be a mate, not in the true sense of the word. You're blushing again, Danica," she observed. "I don't mean just physical intimacy. I mean comfort, and trust. Enjoying someone's company, and being soothed by their nearness. I suppose I mean love. Or if love is impossible, then friendship."

She shook her head, then continued gamely. "I see the way Zane looks at you when he thinks no one is watching. When we first began to speak about this, he told me flatly that he could never love a woman with feathers in her hair. But I watch him now, and . . . he was wrong. He cares about you. And that makes it harder, I think, whenever you pull away from him."

He frightened me sometimes, unnerved me often, but I didn't hate him. Zane was trying so hard for this peace, and having what he was feeling put to me so bluntly was dreadful. Meekly, I stated, "Zane mostly avoids me now. He seems to go out of his way to make sure we are not alone together."

"He doesn't want to push you." Irene sighed, and added, "Look, Zane was on his way to the market a few minutes ago, to haggle prices and settle disputes and other busywork that, for reasons beyond my comprehension, he actually enjoys. Join him there, and I promise he won't turn you away. Give him a chance and see what happens."

Suddenly Irene yawned and made a shooing gesture. "Go rake somewhere, hawk," she said affectionately. "Tell me how it turns out in the morning."

CHAPTER 17

I DID AS IRENE HAD SUGGESTED, AND RE-
turned to the market, where shopkeepers directed me to Zane without my needing to ask.
Someone near him drew his attention to me and
I saw him tense for a moment before he turned
around. I wondered whether he was thinking
about Adelina.

"My exquisite Danica," Zane greeted me,
pulling me into a soft embrace in the marketplace. I lingered in his arms for a few long moments. Zane and I had perfected the appearance
of an infatuated young couple. I was almost
growing used to the little touches—a hand
brushing a hand, his tendency to tuck loose
golden hairs back from my face—that Zane
added so easily to the play.

Remembering Irene's words, I wondered now if what I had taken to be a flawless act might really be more. It had been so long since we had been alone together, it was hard to know for sure.

Was I to blame for that distance?

"Danica, you must know Fisk?" Zane said lightly, referring to the metalworker he had been speaking with.

I did; Fisk Falchion was an avian man from the Aurita who had requested to trade in the serpiente market. There were serpents in our market now also, including a maker of the fine flutes used to accompany serpiente dance.

"Always a pleasure to see you," Fisk greeted me.

"The trade is going well?" I inquired.

Fisk nodded. "There were a few trouble-makers earlier, but they hurried off when Zane came by to speak to me," he answered. "I don't think they will be back soon." Fisk smiled, an expression of fatigue and contentment combined. "The market here is quite impressive. I had not thought it would be so."

Bidding Fisk good day, Zane and I continued to walk in the market. "The Aurita has always been one of my favorite shops," I confided. "I'm glad Fisk was brave enough to take a chance trading here."

"He's a businessman," Zane said with obvious pride. "Our market is not famous for its jewelers, but our people are known for their love of beauty. For a man like Fisk, such an opportunity must have been the dream of a lifetime."

"Do none of the guard follow you here?" I had not seen any since I had gone looking for Adelina earlier.

Zane shook his head. "It's unnecessary. The market sometimes gets a bit rowdy, but I've never had any trouble. Very few people would risk hitting their Diente even in the hottest temper, and if it occurs, I can defend myself in a casual brawl." He added, "They are fond of you, Danica. I've had people come up to me, surprised at how much they like you. That being the case, my people— *your* people—will protect you from anyone who means you harm. Bringing the guard would cause more trouble than it is worth, because it would tell the people that I do not trust them."

THE REST OF the afternoon passed with safe, neutral conversation about pointless things like the price of ivory and how Chinese-style furniture was coming into fashion among both avian and serpiente craftsmen. We drifted from stall to stall, presented with free samples at every stop. I knew that Zane rarely dined in the palace hall for lunch, though I usually joined Irene and Charis there. After sampling the wares of every baker and chef who insisted on feeding us, I wished I had skipped the formal meal, too.

I pleaded an overfull stomach to avoid offending the chef who offered a taste of roast lamb fresh from the fire. Once we were beyond the hearing of the merchant, Zane said, "I've always wondered why you don't eat meat. I understand not wanting to dine on poultry, but even a natural hawk eats small game."

"My great-grandmother Tuuli Thea Caylan could not stand the smell of cooked meat," I explained, recalling the story. "She refused to let it be served in the Keep. Naturally, the cooks learned how to make dishes that Caylan would allow, and now meat is so uncommon in the Keep that I never acquired a taste for it."

Zane appeared genuinely amused. "How utterly odd. Understand this means I must force you to try." He paused, as if considering which of the many merchants prepared the best dish.

"Zane—"

"Now, now." He led me back to the chef who had offered me the lamb a few minutes before. "If you've no moral or religious obligation against it, I cannot allow you to be closed-minded enough not to sample one of this wonderful cook's fine creations."

The "wonderful cook" in question looked very flattered, and I had no doubt that he would have handed over the entire stand free of charge had Zane implied he wanted it.

"What is your masterpiece today?" Zane asked, his expression animated with mischief.

The chef did not hesitate to reply, "I've a wonderful piece of lamb simmered with wine and rosemary that I'm sure your Naga would enjoy."

I resigned myself to tasting the cook's food, knowing that even if it was awful I would need to swallow and smile or else break the poor man's heart. Tentatively, I took the offered morsel and tried not to laugh as both Zane and the chef watched me intently for my reaction.

Come now, Danica, I scolded myself. *You've walked onto the dais in the synkal, and now you need to gather your nerve to put food in your mouth?*

Appropriately chastised, I tasted the lamb.

Though like nothing I had ever eaten before, it was delicious. My surprise must have shown on my face, for the chef grinned and even Zane smiled slightly.

"Does the lady like it?" the chef inquired, though he doubtless knew the answer.

"Wonderful," I answered honestly. "Very . . . strange, but wonderful."

Zane wrapped an arm around my waist and pulled me close, a playful half-hug. "My brave Naga Danica," he said, lightly teasing. To the cook he added, "We will be going back to the Hawk's Keep tomorrow morning, but perhaps next time we are here you might be willing to prepare supper for the family?"

The chef was stunned. "I would be honored, milord. Thank you."

Zane shook his head. "My thanks."

WE DID NOT leave the market until after the sun had set. I could not imagine wanting supper after all I had eaten, and so I was glad when Zane passed by the dining hall with only a brief word of greeting to the occupants and a bid good night.

Zane's mood was still cheerful, but I felt some of the humor fade to contemplation as we walked in silent company back to our rooms.

"Your room, milady," Zane said, with an attempt at lightness, as he opened my door for me. He drew me into a soft embrace as he had in the market, one of those delicate touches he seemed to bestow without thinking.

Was it true that, beneath the volatile exterior I had come to know, he was as hurt and maybe even as scared as I was? Recalling my conversation with Irene, I was determined not to chase him off tonight.

I felt the gentle pressure as Zane kissed my hair. This was the point at which I normally would have pulled away, but I forced myself to relax. Zane seemed to feel my acquiescence; he skimmed his fingers over my cheek and jaw, and tilted my face up.

He had kissed me before—as a challenge to my guards in the Mistari encampment, when I had thought myself to be sleeping, in the synkal in front of his people, before Adelina strode in the morning after the ceremony declaring me Naga.

Now when his lips touched mine, the gesture was as intense as the time in my own bedroom at the Keep, but as leisurely as the slow kiss we had shared in his. When I did not call a stop, he pressed a hand to my lower back, pulling me closer.

My hands had risen instinctively and had been resting on his shoulders as if I would push him back. I made the tight muscles loosen, and felt my hands flutter uncertainly.

Zane's lips moved to lay a brief kiss at the bend between my shoulder and neck, and then another just over my collarbone.

I had a moment's thought, as vivid as it was brief, of a cobra's fangs sinking into the skin his lips touched. For a moment I felt myself tense, pulling away fractionally, and I felt Zane hesitate, frozen for an instant.

"I'm sorry." I didn't mean to say the words, wasn't sure what I was saying them for.

Zane raised his face, and despite my intent, I flinched at the expression in his garnet gaze, which had the heat of anger and the sharpness of pain and yet was somehow neither of those.

Just as unexpected was the sensation of falling as he released me, almost throwing himself back as he spun away. He tumbled awkwardly to his knees, breathing hard, until his forehead leaned against the wall.

Frightened and confused by the sudden withdrawal, I knelt by his side.

He recoiled and rose to his feet with the gracefully controlled violence of a serpiente soldier on the field. I froze when I saw his eyes flashing not with annoyance or amusement but anger, directed at me.

One, two, three paces backward, and then he turned from me, and I could tell he was going to leave me alone in my confusion.

It hurt to see him draw back from me, and I fought every instinct not to hide behind the comfortable reserve I knew so well. "Zane—"

He turned back to me and took a deep breath, his gaze holding me in place, frozen, as if I had met the gorgon's eyes, except for the frantic beat of my heart. "I do appreciate the effort, Danica. I enjoyed spending time with you in the market, and I'm glad to see you can be so comfortable around my people. But you're here alone with me now only despite your fear . . . and I'm not looking for that kind of sacrifice." His voice softened as his anger simmered out. "I would be your lover if you would trust me, but I don't want you to come to me because you feel like it is an . . . unpleasant duty. I would rather be your enemy than a meaningless obligation."

My heart lurched into my throat at his words, and for a moment all I could do was stand dumbly. By the time I had unraveled my tongue to argue, he was continuing, the last of his rage gone.

"If you want to make the offer someday when it means something to you . . ." He shrugged, and for a moment the brilliant, charm-birds-from-their-nests smile was back, but then he was gone and I stood in shock.

He is wrong. Whatever else our relationship might be, it could never be meaningless.

Heart still beating loud enough to wake the dead, I followed him into the hall, trying to discern which direction he had gone. In that moment of hesitation, my ears picked up a noise that registered as subtly wrong.

The sound came again: a familiar cry that raised the feathers on the back of my neck. Carefully but quickly I moved toward it.

Just a few paces beyond the hallway's bend, I saw two figures fighting. One was obviously Zane; his movements had the frightening fluidity of a serpiente warrior, and he fought as soundlessly as all his people. The only noise came from his opponent, and even that was so soft I would never have heard it had I not stopped in the hall.

The second figure was either a slender young

man or a plain, shapeless female; I suspected the first. The loose black clothing he wore left much to the imagination—as much as the silken scarf twined around the assassin's head, which showed only shadows over his eyes.

The word *assassin* came to my mind unbidden, but as soon as I thought it, I knew it to be true. I also knew, from the style of his movements, that the attacker was probably avian. He was fighting with the long-bladed dirk many of the Royal Flight favored, and he guarded his back with the precision of a soldier who is used to defending wings.

Quickly my thoughts shifted. If the assassin was avian, caution made it reasonable to assume the blade of his weapon was poisoned. Depending on the strength, a scratch could kill; he did not even need to land a fatal blow.

I did not wait for an opportunity. Against avian poison, I was safer than Zane, and I hoped that even an assassin would hesitate to harm his Tuuli Thea. All but ignoring the weapon, I grasped the attacker from behind and dragged him backward to keep Zane from the range of his blade.

The assassin whirled, and I raised an arm to defend my face. I felt the knife cut through the flesh of my forearm and the heat of poison in the wound, but I also felt my attacker recoil. He had recognized me.

Obviously unwilling to continue the fight

with me in the middle, the assassin spun and took off down the hall.

Zane moved as if to follow, but then he turned to me.

"Danica, are you okay?"

I was going to say yes, I think, but at that moment the world warped and churned around me, and I stumbled back into the wall. Zane gathered me in his arms and hurried to pound on a doorway down the hall. Almost instantly four of the guard emerged.

"Adelina, we've had a run-in with an assassin, avian, I think. Danica's hurt. He went in the direction of the north exit."

Adelina nodded sharply. "You, with me," she ordered one of her men, who I recognized as Irene's mate, Galen. To the other two she said quickly, "You, stay with your Diente, and you, fetch the doctor and Danica's guard. Keep quiet," she added, with a glance at Zane that lingered only a moment too long. "We don't want this hollered all over the palace."

"Let's get her back to her room," Adelina suggested, speaking to Zane, who nodded mutely. She added, "We wouldn't have moments like this if you shouted when attacked."

Zane shook off the criticism. "The injury isn't bad, but . . ."

Time warped a bit right then. The next thing I knew, Andreios was bandaging my arm while the doctor paced in the background. "It won't kill her," I heard Rei explaining to Zane, "but— Danica, how do you feel?" he asked, noticing I was awake.

"Not well," I responded. My throat felt dry.

"You'll be fine," he assured me. "The poison must have been nearly pure to affect you this strongly, but it isn't designed to harm avians. You'll probably drift in and out for a while, and after that you might suffer dizzy spells for a couple . . ."

Again the words trailed off.

The next time I woke, I was lying on my bed, still in the palace. Zane was sitting beside me.

"Water?" he offered.

"Please." He wrapped an arm under my shoulders to help me sit up, and I gulped down the drink he held to my lips.

"You could have been killed." His voice was carefully neutral, the same tone with which he had offered water, and I wondered what emotion he was trying not to share.

I shook my head, and that made it spin. A deep breath grounded me, and when I was sure I was not about to pass out again, I added, "I assumed one of my people would hesitate to hurt me. Even a scratch from that knife would have *killed* you."

"How were you so sure it was one of yours?" Zane answered.

"The way he moved. Did they catch him?"

"*Her*," Zane corrected. "The guard cornered the girl down the hall." He paused reflectively and then admitted, "It surprised me, too, that she was one of my people."

"Serpent?" I thought back and remembered how the would-be assassin had fought. "But she moved as if she had avian training."

"She might have been a dancer; a good one of that guild could probably imitate an avian fighter. My guess is that she was trying to return us to war. According to Andreios, one of the Royal Flight had his weapon stolen recently. Our serpent either didn't realize how strong the poison was, or she was willing to kill me. Any observer would have blamed the murder on your people, and that would have caused havoc."

"Have you spoken with the . . . her?" I could not make myself say "assassin" aloud.

Zane shook his head. "According to Adelina, she took her own life when she realized the guard had her cornered."

My head was spinning again, and I put a hand to my temple as if that might keep the world still. "What was her name?"

"It wasn't in Adelina's report," Zane answered. "Only that the girl was a viper. Probably no one in the guard recognized her."

"Did you . . . see her?" I asked.

"No." His gaze flickered as if he was uncertain

about that decision. "If none of the guard recognized her, I suppose I wouldn't have, either. They can deal with the body. I preferred to stay here to make sure you would be all right." Regarding me critically, he said, "You should probably rest more."

"How long did Rei say it would be until I am on my feet again?" I asked as Zane helped me to lie down again.

"Not much longer," he answered. "This is the most lucid you've been since you were hurt."

"How long ago was that?"

"Almost a full day. Close your eyes, Danica. Try to rest."

I did as I was bidden, and almost instantly I was asleep.

CHAPTER 18

ZANE DID NOT MOVE MORE THAN TWO
steps from my side when I was finally well
enough to walk about. My stomach was still feeling picky, so the lamb dinner was further delayed, but aside from an occasional few moments
of faintness, I felt fine.

"Are you sure you're okay to travel?" Zane
asked. It was the hundredth time I had heard the
question that day. Rei had asked as many times as
Zane.

"I'm fine." I sighed again. "We're already late
arriving at the Keep, and I don't want anyone
imagining I've been killed over here."

Both Rei and Zane had to agree with that
reasoning. With one of them on each side of me,
we rode.

IT WAS A hard trip, but Rei had insisted that riding was safer than flying if I was still having dizzy spells. By the time we arrived, I had gained a new appreciation for how much time Zane had spent traveling this path by horse while I held to the luxury of flight.

At the entrance to the Keep, we were met by a flurry of the Royal Flight, led by Gerard in Rei's absence. Near the edge of the group was a worn-looking Erica Silvermead. She did not even seem to have the heart to give Zane a proper glare as we dismounted in the courtyard.

Gerard filled us in quietly as the horses were stabled. "Erica returned to duty a few hours ago. Her father's death has taken a toll on her. A few weeks ago, he would have been listed as a soldier in battle; now he has been labeled a traitor."

The words made me take a second look at the young sparrow who stood across the courtyard like a lost soul. She was slender, hated the serpiente and had been out of sight the past several days.

Rei caught me examining the girl with a critical eye. "Adelina caught the assassin," he said, sensing my thoughts. "But if you are still worried, I can keep a closer eye on Erica." The offer made it clear that he too was concerned about Erica's state of mind.

"Thank you," I answered.

"Shardae, did you intend to loiter in the courtyard for hours while I wondered over your whereabouts?" I turned toward my mother, feeling appropriately chastised. However, beneath the censure, her face and voice both betrayed worry. "You have been missed these last few days, and the market and court are both full of nasty rumors. Karashan was on the verge of storming the palace, sure you had been abducted or worse."

"We had some problems with a . . . would-be assassin," I answered hesitantly. I went on to explain as much of the circumstances as was my mother's business, including the fact that while the assassin had imitated an avian soldier, Adelina had reported her to be a serpent.

My mother gasped. "Did it not even occur to you that you might have been the target?"

I shook my head. "I wasn't. There was plenty of opportunity to harm me."

She frowned. "If your theory is correct that someone is trying to start the war again," she pressed, ignoring Zane completely as she spoke, "then why would a serpent have hesitated to harm you? In the heart of the serpiente palace, that would have caused as much trouble as if she had killed your alistair."

"I don't know." I glanced at Zane, wondering if he had thought this point through.

"My best guess is that she wasn't trying to kill anyone," he offered. "She was trying to make it appear as if someone had attempted to kill me, but she probably balked at actually doing the deed."

"Nice to know your kind hesitates at some crimes," my mother said dryly. "The idea still seems unlikely to me. You are certain that this Adelina didn't make a mistake?"

"Do you have a better theory?" I spoke a bit louder than was necessary and gave Zane a warning glance before he could say the caustic remark that was surely waiting on the tip of his tongue.

My mother made some reply along the lines of "I will consider it," but I did not truly heed the words. I grasped at Zane's arm, trying to remain standing as one of the now familiar waves of dizziness passed over me.

"Shardae, for the love of sunlight, go lie down." My mother's voice finally came fully to my ears. "You're frighteningly pale. Why in the world did you let her travel in this condition?" This last was demanded of Rei.

"She insisted" was his answer. "Your daughter did not want you to worry."

"I'm fine, Mother." I even managed to release Zane and remain on my feet. "The spells are not nearly as bad now as they were earlier."

My mother shook her head skeptically. "Danica, you must have ridden for hours just to get here, on top of having been injured. If your guards and your alistair cannot convince you, then allow me to appeal to your sanity. Go lie down."

I nodded finally. It *was* late, and I had ridden hard. "Fine, I will go."

"Zane, perhaps you might stay?" my mother asked as we turned to leave. "I have a question for you regarding your people down in the market. There's no trouble—Danica, please, go to bed," she interrupted herself when I paused. "This is hardly anything important enough to warrant your attention."

"Sleep well, Danica," Zane said, already turning to speak to my mother.

I knew she was just trying to keep Zane away from me. Anything "hardly important enough" for me to be bothered with was surely nothing Zane needed to hear at this moment. She wanted to make sure I would go to my room alone.

I slept poorly, with a scattering of dreams I could not quite remember, yet I woke when dawn was barely brushing the sky, feeling surprisingly refreshed.

I did not want to bother any of the Keep servants yet, so I slipped into clean clothing and padded into the hall unaccompanied.

Rei had been on duty guarding the hall, and at the moment he was deep in conversation with Zane.

"I wish I could," Rei interrupted whatever Zane had been saying, his voice slightly raised. "If you—"

"Danica." I had been seen. Zane cut off Rei's words and stepped past my guard to greet me. "Good morning. How are you feeling?"

"Fine . . . good. What were you two talking about this early?" The instant I asked the question, Rei's expression let me know they had been talking about me. In what context, I did not know.

"Idle fantasies," Zane answered smoothly. Neither his voice nor his face gave away his thoughts. However, I trusted Rei implicitly and knew that he would not have tolerated insults or threats against me. "Andreios has been telling me avian lore."

That I could believe. Andreios had a passion for the old stories that belied his otherwise reserved nature. When prompted, he spun the mythical origins of our kind in a way that could make the hardest skeptic believe for a moment that they were real.

As we descended the stairs toward the court, Rei made most of the conversation. "I spoke to Lady Nacola," he commented. "In light of the attempt on Zane's life at the palace, she has dropped her argument against allowing some of his guard into the Keep. Adelina and Ailbhe should arrive before dawn tomorrow morning, and I've asked them to report to me when they do so." Rei shrugged lightly as he commented, "Your mother wavers between threatening Zane's life and trying to preserve it. She's convinced that our people were somehow involved in the attack at the palace."

"Adelina's coming?" The words were sharper than I had intended; Zane's expression took on the barest hint of a frown.

I doubted that Rei was as oblivious to the tension as he appeared, but he answered, "She is the captain of the guard, and is more than capable in that capacity. In addition to her technical qualifications, she seems very loyal."

Rei's opinion sealed the matter. He was captain of the Royal Flight, and if he thought Adelina would benefit the Keep, I would have to accept his decision.

Though the formal breakfast would not be served for hours, fruit, bread, milk and cider were available in the court for early risers. Several such people greeted us quietly before returning to what they were doing.

I helped myself to an ample meal. My appetite had finally returned, and it had done so with a vengeance. Though Rei had already eaten, Zane served himself a meal similar to mine, and we sat at one of the side tables to eat.

"What did my mother have to say about our flute-maker last night?" I asked Zane, trying to draw him from the melancholy silence he seemed to have fallen into.

He smiled wryly, and the expression appeared forced. "Nothing important, really. I think she doesn't like the thought of my having time on my hands in which I can plan mischief."

Rei glanced at me quizzically, clearly asking whether he should leave. I didn't like seeing Zane in this mood and wanted a moment alone with Rei to ask what they had been discussing that had bothered the serpiente so much.

He made up his mind without input from me. Standing, Rei apologized. "I need to check in with my flight to make sure there won't be trouble when Adelina and Ailbhe get here tomorrow. Karl will be with you today," he added, nodding toward the doorway, where the slender raven waited unobtrusively. Quietly, so only Zane and I would hear, Rei added, "Karl's weapon was the one stolen by your serpiente assassin, and he has been doing everything he can to earn back my flight's confidence. I've never had a problem with him before; he's one of my most competent soldiers, and he is infinitely loyal. You can trust him."

With this reassurance, Rei left, and Zane and I picked at our food in silence. I made a few more attempts at conversation, to which Zane responded with what sounded like a forced attempt at lightness.

Eventually I gave up on discretion and asked point-blank, "Zane, what's wrong?"

"Why would I be bothered by anything?" he replied sarcastically. "I was nearly killed within five steps of my own bedroom, and you were injured. What one person does, several people usually consider—several people who, in this case, are considering what the benefits would be if you or I met with an untimely death." He stood from the table, and I could see he was trying to gather his self-control. "Excuse me, Danica. I shouldn't be sharp with you, of all people."

"In this situation, it's perfectly forgivable."

He just shook his head.

THOUGH ZANE MADE every attempt to hide it, his dark mood persisted for the rest of the day. In front of avians who had not spent as much time with him as I had recently, he must have simply seemed more subdued than usual—a favorable turn in the eyes of the court, with which we spent most of the day.

The two serpiente merchants, however, exchanged worried glances during the short conversation they had with Zane and me while we were circuiting the market.

"It has been a trying few days," Zane apologized as he excused himself early that evening.

The sky was well past dark and court had begun to tire when I politely followed Zane's lead. I wanted to talk to him, but what would I say? I did care for him in a way; it had not only been a fear for the peace that had prompted me to drag the assassin away from him. But I knew that wary affection was not what he sought and would bring him little comfort.

After several hours of tossing and turning in my own bed, I flew to the fifth floor and knocked lightly on Andreios's door.

Rei did not appear surprised to see me; he invited me into his study, bidding me to close the door behind me.

"You're worried about Zane," he predicted before I attempted to raise the subject. I had confided in Rei most of my life; I valued his advice even more than my mother's.

"He's been . . . tense for weeks," I admitted, hedging around the real problem, "but never so moody as he was today. You two were speaking about something this morning, something that upset him. Can you tell me what?"

"Fate," Rei answered after a moment. I could tell that the conversation was eating away at him as surely as it had been Zane. He paused, took a moment to gather his words and then asked bluntly, "Do you love him?"

The question startled me. "No." I did not need to think about the answer, which sounded so brutal that I needed to add, "I do not hate him anymore, but love . . . I believe he deserves love. But I don't know if I can be the one to give it."

"Do you trust him?"

"I trust his intentions," I answered, trying to be as honest as possible.

"But do you trust *him*?" Rei pressed. "If you were falling, would you trust him to catch you? Would you trust him never to harm you, no matter what he could gain? Would you trust him to risk his own life for yours, without hesitation?"

I had to shake my head.

I respected Zane, which seemed odd, when for so many years I had only known his name as a curse. But I knew that while we danced with peace, we were both still prepared to fight. If I was falling, I trusted he would catch me—unless it was a choice between me or one of his own people. I trusted him to never harm me, because harming me would destroy this peace—unless I reneged on this deal and my death was necessary. As for risking his life for mine . . . his people needed a king.

I found myself pacing in a most unladylike fashion. Then I stopped, not because Rei ever objected to my un-avian outbursts, but because I thought of Zane asking me not to hide.

Rei sighed. "He said that you were passionate, that he was amazed by how much you could care even for someone you didn't know but to fear."

"And he said," Rei continued, as if the words came painfully to him, "that you deserved love. That you deserved someone . . . with whom you could cry or laugh without hiding your face."

I winced at the words, closing my eyes as they rocked me. I needed to speak to Zane. I might make a fool out of myself, but I needed to. . . . In the next moment I felt Rei's arms around me, a warm comfort.

"I love you." He whispered the words against my hair like an apology, but within them was surrender. For him, the battle was already lost.

I looked up, though I didn't know what I wanted to say, and Rei's lips gently caressed mine. Time hung suspended for long moments, during which my heart couldn't decide whether to sink into my stomach or lodge in my throat, but then I started to pull away. *Zane.*

The door opened behind me, and we jumped apart. I spun around, and heat flushed my cheeks as the expressions on both of the intruders' faces made it very clear what they thought the situation to be.

Karl quickly averted his eyes while he fought to control his shock. Adelina was furious.

Karl spoke before any of us could. "She . . . I—" He swallowed heavily before deciding to ignore what he had seen and spoke to Rei. "Sir, Adelina is here. You wished to have her report to you immediately?"

Adelina's eyes flashed at Andreios. "I didn't realize I'd be disturbing you." Her voice was taut with anger. "Should I come back later?"

"You didn't interrupt anything," Rei answered firmly. "Karl, please escort Shardae back to her rooms. Adelina, I can show you to your room if you would like to rest a bit, or you can have the full tour of the Keep now."

"I would prefer to know the layout of this place before I sleep," Adelina replied caustically. "There seems to be no telling what goes on here."

I heard the words behind me as I walked out, suddenly feeling pale. Nothing had happened, and nothing would have happened, but I doubted Adelina would believe that.

CHAPTER 19

WE RETURNED TO THE SERPIENTE PALACE A few days later. I found myself watching Zane closely for signs that Adelina had told him what she had seen, but in the flurry of activity surrounding the upcoming holiday, she and the incident both seemed to fade into the background.

I sought out the dancer A'isha during any free time I had, and she taught me a few simple steps, sensual and exotic dances that I doubted I would ever have the courage to perform—until the sun rose on the day of the fall equinox and the serpiente lands were suddenly perfumed with sweets and spices, and the air rippled with the sounds of flutes and two-toned drums.

Unfortunately, the Namir-da was still far

beyond me. A'isha's words on the subject were, "Perhaps you might learn it, in more time. You have talent, but . . . not much practice."

Throughout the day, serpiente spilled into the marketplace, their bodies, skins and belongings decorated with enough color, scent and texture to boggle the mind.

I had barely stepped into the market with Zane at my side before one of the dancers that A'isha and I had practiced with offered me a gold and crimson silk scarf called a *melos*, the ends of which were strung with dozens of tiny golden bells.

According to A'isha, the *melos* was given to dancers as both praise for their skill and a request for a performance. Zane made a move as if to decline for me, not expecting me to know the meaning of the gift, but I tugged it from his grasp. Then I did a few steps from one from the dances I knew, and saw Zane's eyes widen with shock.

Laughing a little, I moved a few steps ahead; Zane answered the challenge, and within moments we had been ushered onto one of the many daises that stood in the market. Aside from A'isha, I had never performed for an audience before. Now I met Zane's gaze and took a deep breath to steady myself.

I inhaled the festive air of the Namir-da, and we danced.

In a society that worships love, freedom and beauty, dance is sacred. It is a prayer for the future, a remembrance of the past and a joyful exclamation of thanks for the present.

Zane and I danced several times in the marketplace throughout the day. When we ran out of dances I knew, we improvised. When we were hungry or thirsty, all we needed to do was step down from the stage and we were offered more than our fill.

The day started to wane, and a circular dais was constructed in the synkal, ten paces across in every direction and a few inches higher than Zane could reach while standing on his toes. The dais had no railing, and as night fell it was lit only by the torches that burned on the floor all around it.

Finally, as the last rays of the sunset faded, I took my seat with Charis at the back of the stage as Zane spoke to the assembled crowd. With words as vibrant as paintings, he told the story of Maeve and Kiesha, of the cult of Anhamirak, of Maeve's seduction and of Leben's gifts to her and her people.

When he had finished, the doors opened in the back of the synkal. The children were escorted out to the market, where they would stay up late into the evening enjoying candies, games and magic.

The adults stayed, and when the palace guard doused all the torches in the room but those around the dais, everyone turned to Irene and Galen as they prepared to dance—everyone except Charis.

I felt her tense, but when I looked to her, she was staring off the stage at someone in the darkness. Abruptly she stood, dragging me up with her. Zane heard the movement and his head whipped around toward us.

Yet every one of these actions was a second too late.

I was struck with a pain so fierce I could not even cry out; a brutal tearing constricted my lungs and sent ripples of crimson across my vision.

Charis collapsed beside me; I felt her weight on me, and I started to fall, but then Zane caught us both. In complete silence he carried us off the stage and into the relative safety of the hall.

Beyond that, my memories are scattered.

Zane's telling the guard to make sure Irene and Galen were safe, and to lock the doors. The assassin was inside.

Zane's white face as he leaned over me, telling me I would be fine. Begging me to stay awake with him.

Andreios's normally bronzed skin, turned a sickly ashen green. His turning to Zane and shaking his head.

"No." Zane's tone was flat, as if in shock. "That's impossible."

Rei's ordering, "Someone get him out of here." The guards looking at each other, wondering who to obey. A figure being dragged away.

"You can go to sleep now," Irene said. She was still dressed in the glittering black and silver dress she had danced in. Her face was pale, and her hands were shaking.

I slept, and when I woke next, the pain was less. There were bandages wrapped around my torso. Andreios was by my side.

"Thank the sky you're awake."

"I seem to keep being poisoned." The words took all my scant air, and when I tried to draw a deep breath, the pain struck.

"You'll be okay," Rei told me. "But it will take a while for you to heal. You've had a narrow escape—any higher, and the arrow would have hit your lung. Lower would have been just as bad."

"Arrow?"

"It was avian-style, but it must have been shot from a serpiente bow—the wound is deep. You've been out for almost a full day now.... We weren't sure you were ever going to wake." On the last words his voice betrayed his fear.

Suddenly my fuzzy mind put together those last painful moments. My mouth was dry when I asked, "Charis?"

"It just barely nicked her arm, but ..." He looked away. "She was unconscious before Zane carried the two of you to the hall, and she still hasn't woken. I don't think she will."

"Is Zane—" I stopped, needing to carefully draw more breath.

"Sleeping, right now," Rei answered. Wryly, he confessed, "The guard drugged him."

Someone knocked quietly on the door. "Come in," Rei called. "She's awake."

Irene Cobriana entered. Her steps dragged slightly, and her eyes were swollen as if she had been crying, but she held her head high.

"Irene, you should be lying down," Rei chastised lightly.

"I can't sleep anymore," she answered. "I came to see how Danica was doing."

I tried a smile, but was not sure whether it worked. "Can't get rid of me ... that easily."

"Andreios was supposed to call me as soon as you were awake, but I suspected he wouldn't,"

Irene said, with what was supposed to be levity but did not quite make the mark. "If you think you can eat, there's some rather unattractive green broth you're supposed to try."

I looked at Rei, who nodded solemnly. "It's very . . . healthy, I'm sure. The Keep and palace doctors worked together to concoct it. I suspect it will taste terrible."

He was correct.

Lunch was another strange-colored liquid; this time it was gray. By dinnertime cooks had intervened, so it was a warm vegetable broth that the doctors had added their medicines to. It numbed the pain and allowed me to sleep.

I woke at odd hours, ate what was forced upon me and then slept again.

I had no idea how much time passed. I did not know what day it was when I finally woke to find Zane by my bedside.

"Zane—"

"How do you feel?"

I paused to catalog my pains, which were few at that moment. There was a curious tingle around my injury, which I suspected would turn into a throbbing pain if I tried to move. "I don't know."

Zane smiled wistfully, but then the expression faded. "My mother is dead," he said without preamble. "She died last night."

I tried to form words, but nothing was

enough. "She tried to save me," I told him, knowing the words only spoke my own pain and could never heal his. "She tried to pull me out of the way."

"I know," Zane answered, his voice dead of emotion. "If you had both remained seated, the arrow probably would have hit you in the throat, and then her in the side. It would have killed you both.

"It doesn't make any sense, you know," Zane continued. "Even if they could have gotten into the synkal without being seen, and they didn't intend for you to be hit, no loyal avian would have risked your life that way. And no one loyal to the Cobriana would have used poison that wouldn't hurt you but would kill any of my family it nicked."

"Zane, are you all right?" Through the entire speech, his face had remained expressionless.

"I'm quite sure I'm not," he answered evenly. "But I'm alive, and uninjured, and—" I reached for his hand, and finally I heard his voice choke off, as his fragile shell cracked. "Danica, I've never been this frightened in my life." The words spilled out in a flood of emotion. "The guard made the announcement about my mother this morning, and right now people are still in shock. I don't know how they'll respond when they wake up from it. . . ." He took a deep breath, and then said on a rush of air, "I think it must have

225

been one of my guard who made the shot, or at least who organized it."

"What?" Instinctively I tried to sit up, and the pain returned abruptly, a spear driven into my gut, just below the left side of my ribcage.

"Careful, Danica," Zane cautioned, wincing.

"Tell me . . . about the guard." After that, he could get the doctors and they could drug me to sleep again, but first I wanted answers.

"It would have been nearly impossible for an avian to be in the crowd unnoticed. Weapons aren't allowed in the synkal anyway, and a serpiente bow is not easily concealed. Only one of my guards could have managed it."

"But the poison?" The question was short. Longer sentences took up more breath than I could get comfortably.

Zane shook his head. "I don't know. Maybe they stole it."

"How?" As I asked the question, I knew the answer. Adelina and Ailbhe both had been to the Keep. Either of them could have sneaked a bow into the synkal. Either of them would have known when the lights would go out. "But Charis . . . They wouldn't hurt her."

"There was bad blood between Adelina's family and mine for generations. My mother was the first to allow one of them into the guard, the first to trust them, and for that they were more than grateful. I can't imagine *any* of the guard being willing to hurt my mother, but I believe any one of them would before Adelina and Ailbhe." Zane shook his head, running fingers restlessly through his hair. "Andreios tells me they weren't allowed near the storeroom, anyway, and that the poison was too strong for them to have taken it from his people; it had to be mixed just for this occasion. Only someone in the Royal Flight would have had the access necessary to make the poison, but any of them would have used an avian bow. Besides, an avian who was willing to plot assassination would not have aimed at my mother; he would have gone for me." He sighed and leaned against the bed, his entire frame drooping with fatigue. "As I said, it doesn't make any sense."

My nurse, a shy little sparrow who had accompanied the Keep's doctor here, interrupted us at that point. "Milady, would you like supper?" she asked politely.

I tried to decline, but Zane would not let me. He sat on the opposite side of the bed and amused us with quaint stories as I swallowed every drop of the foul concoction. I was almost asleep before the nurse had closed the door behind her.

Zane kissed my forehead lightly, as if I was a child. "Sleep, Danica."

CHAPTER 20

THOUGH MY KIND HEALS AT A RATE THAT would seem miraculous to any human doctor, when one is bedridden, nothing ever seems fast enough.

My mother was wary about coming to the palace herself and insisted that she needed to stay at the Keep, but she sent sparrow messengers at least once a day demanding reports on my progress. She also made sure that I had the best avian doctors in the land tending to me.

Zane rarely left my side. Occasionally he would go out to the market while I slept and arrange for dancers, magicians and musicians to entertain me, but he was always beside me as I drifted into sleep and when I woke.

Clothed in deep violet, the serpiente color of

mourning, Zane was no less elegant than he had ever been. However, there was something fragile about his movements, a fatigue no amount of sleep could cure.

Before his people, he put on a good front. Though somber, he still appeared strong and confident. I saw the mask every time someone came to visit me, and I watched it fall every time they left, as if it exhausted him to enact the play his position demanded.

One evening I woke to a sound I could not quite place. When I finally recognized it, I felt a pain sharper then the arrow that had torn into me.

Zane was crying. His back was to me, and he was leaning against the wall with his head in his hands. His shoulders shook as he tried not to make a sound.

"Zane."

"I'm sorry." His voice was muffled.

"You're allowed to cry." He still didn't turn toward me. "Zane, please, come here."

His chest rose and fell with each deep breath as he fought to gather his composure and put one foot in front of the other until he reached me.

I pushed myself up, ignoring the twinge in my side. My pain was tolerable; his was not.

"I didn't mean to wake you," he apologized again.

Zane, whose face was smudged with shadows

and wet with tears, hadn't meant to wake *me*. I wondered when last he had slept a night through.

I reached to brush the tears from his face; Zane turned toward the touch, closing his eyes.

Using the shelf beside my bed for support, I pulled myself to my feet. Standing was difficult, but manageable.

Zane caught my arm and steadied me. "Danica—"

I cut off his words with two fingertips against his lips, to which he planted a gossamer kiss.

Uncertain why, but with no thought of why *not*, I drew his face down to mine. I tasted the salt from his tears as my lips touched briefly against his cheek. Again he closed his eyes, and I kissed each trembling eyelid before finally lowering my lips to his.

Just as tenderly as he had kissed my fingertips, Zane met my lips, unhurried and undemanding.

The kiss was called short by the pain that crept deeper into my side with every moment.

"We both need comfort, and rest," I said. "I can offer one, and the night will provide the other."

Ever so gently, Zane helped me to lie back down. He lay beside me. When I leaned against him, he sighed, kissing my hair, and—mindful of my injury—carefully wrapped an arm around my waist to hold me close.

I rested my cheek against his chest and fell asleep to the gentle rhythm of his breathing and the calm song of his heart. I did not wake again until someone knocked on the door.

"Danica?" a worried voice called.

Zane answered for me, "One minute." He kissed my forehead chastely and then seemed discontented with that and so lowered his lips to mine for a real kiss—one I saw no reason to withhold.

He climbed carefully out of the bed and opened the door for my doctor, an old crow named Betsy, who had been around the Keep since my great-grandmother Caylan's childhood.

"How are you feeling today?" she asked.

I had slept deeply and naturally for the first time in weeks, which made me answer, "Quite well."

"Very good, very good," Betsy answered. "Your mother will be pleased that I finally have something positive to tell her."

The doctor left instructions that I could start on more solid food in a few days, and that I should try to stand up and walk a bit whenever I felt strong enough.

"How do *you* feel?" I asked Zane once we were alone again.

"I don't know." He stopped and shook his head. "My father died when I was a child. I've lost three brothers and a sister since then, and I mourned for each of them. When Gregory died, I decided he would be the last. I was so certain that if I tried, I could keep what was left of my family safe. . . ." He did not need to say more.

I held out a hand to him and he sat beside me.

"I forgot about her, Danica," he confided, and I heard in his voice that this above all was bothering him. "When I pulled the two of you off the stage, there was so much blood on you, and the injury looked so bad . . . I didn't even glance at my mother, didn't . . ." He trailed off again.

I leaned against him, lending my warmth as I spoke. "She was unconscious almost instantly—I felt her fall, Zane," I explained. "There was nothing you could have done."

"I *forgot* about her," he argued.

"You were scared." *As I've been scared before*, I added silently. *So scared I didn't know what to think or do.* "You did all you could."

We passed a while in companionable silence, until Zane whispered finally, "You are so patient with me."

Deciding there was a time to be somber and there was a time to lighten the mood, I responded, "I have to be. . . . I can't walk out without your help."

CHAPTER 21

OVER THE NEXT WEEK I GRADUALLY gained strength, and finally I could take short walks with Zane to the market. I hated to return to my room so early, and delayed as much as possible, until Zane frequently ended up carrying me much of the way back.

If it bothered him, he never complained. When I was tired, he would curl up with me in bed no matter the hour and we would rest together.

I remembered once comparing him to Vasili in my mind, long ago when he had spoken to me in my room in the Keep, but now I could barely see the resemblance. Zane was warm where Vasili had been cool, offering laughter where Vasili would have given a silent smile.

Vasili and I had been betrothed when I was an infant and he was a child of three. In memory, I looked at him through a child's eyes. I loved him—as a father, as a brother, as a mentor.

These thoughts chased themselves through my mind as Zane and I lingered in the serpiente market longer than usual to watch A'isha perform the sakkri. The dance was even more ancient than the sacred Namir-da. According to myth, it had originated in the cult of Anhamirak, where it had been used to summon spirits. The haunting music and elaborate, complex movements almost made it seem like A'isha must have spectral partners dancing with her.

After it was over, I spotted white-blond hair moving through the crowd. Adelina. She approached us timidly, waiting as we both turned to acknowledge her.

"My Naga Danica," she greeted me. I had never heard her address me by title before. "May I speak to you alone for a moment, please?" The guard's expression was anxious enough to put me on edge.

I glanced at Zane, who shrugged slightly. "I can wait here for you. But this is already longer than you've been walking since you were hurt; try not to linger too long."

"I'll be right back."

Adelina led me to a slightly less crowded section of the market. We were by no means "alone," but we had as much privacy as we would find out here.

"I owe you an apology, milady." Her gaze flickered toward Zane. "After the Mistari made their suggestion, I was the one who protested loudest and longest. More than anything, I wanted Zane happy, and I hated that he would give up that happiness for peace." She sighed, shaking her head, obviously having trouble finding the words she needed. "You two had a rocky start, so I suppose it's natural you would seek comfort with someone you are more familiar with."

She hesitated, and I remembered seeing her with Zane and hearing her plead with him as he refused to go against his vows.

I was about to speak, but Adelina continued. "I still hated you for it, when you went to your Rei and Zane wouldn't come to me." I tried to argue and tell her the truth about a scene that must have been eating away at her since she had seen it, but she wouldn't let me. "What's done is done. I've never seen Zane look at a woman like he looks at you now . . . not even me." Her voice held more than a trace of longing as she said the words. "Oh yes, I'm jealous. Perhaps if I were one of your avian guards, I could pretend otherwise, but I don't have their reserve. And . . . you make him happy. So I feel that I should apologize." She added softly, "For more than you know."

"You're . . . forgiven," I answered, finally finding the words to speak.

"You'll be happy to know that I'm retiring from the guard tomorrow," Adelina added. "It doesn't seem appropriate for me to stay. I just—" Her voice broke off in pain.

"Good night, Danica," she whispered before turning away.

I bid her good night, feeling more than a little dazed, and went back to find Zane. I did not repeat Adelina's words to him as we returned to our room; they were personal, and I could not consider telling them to Zane until I understood them myself.

You make him happy. I hoped so.

We lay down together again, side by side. He trailed his fingers through my hair, hesitating for just a moment as they passed between the golden feathers hidden there.

"I don't think I'll ever get used to these," Zane commented, "but they don't bother me nearly so much as they used to."

I smiled, snuggling closer. "Maybe someday I'll take you flying." I imagined growing my Demi-form's wings and lifting Zane into the air.

"As soon as you let A'isha teach you to dance the Namir-da," he challenged. "Until then, my feet will remain firmly on the ground."

Sweetly, I agreed, "Deal." I raised my head, and Zane obligingly met my lips with his own.

"You are too tempting," he whispered.

He wrapped one arm around my waist to hold me close as his other hand skimmed down my side, a light caress that ended at my mid-thigh.

We were at the point where one of us had always backed off before, but I didn't want this to end, not yet.

Zane's hand slid down to my knee, gently moving me so I leaned toward his body. I shifted to accommodate the new position, and with the movement came a spark of pain. The sensation was over instantly, but Zane felt me tense, and thankfully recognized the reason. He sighed, drawing back.

"Don't you dare leave me now."

"You're still healing; I don't want to hurt you." His expression told me that he couldn't believe he was the one saying no this time.

"You won't."

Do you trust him?

When had we reached the point where the answer to Rei's question had become yes without hesitation? When Zane had sat by my bedside for hours while I was drifting in and out of consciousness? When he had arranged for me to be visited by entertainers and friends, or had carried me home when I was too tired to walk? Or when I had first seen him cry and had wanted nothing but to comfort him?

I do not know how, yet somehow, impossibly, we are here.

Zane hesitated, looking at me with temptation and worry in his eyes. The decision was yet unmade when someone pounded on the door, the raps too sharp to be ignored.

Eleanor Lyssia's voice drifted through the door. "Danica, Zane, Rei told me to get you."

Zane swore, pushing himself up, and helped me to my feet. He cast one last lingering look back at the bed before turning toward the door.

Anxiety was written on Eleanor's face. She led us to the main hall, where Andreios met us outside the doors. He had a cut down his left cheek and another one across his ribs. His expression was drawn but not frightened. Still, it was enough to make me queasy with worry.

He nodded toward the closed door of the hall. "We've found our assassins," he said. "Erica and Ailbhe are holding them."

It took a moment for the statement to register. My first thoughts were of Ailbhe and Adelina's treatment of me when I had first entered serpiente land, and of Erica's zealousness against the serpiente. It seemed likely we might end up with only pieces of the assassins left.

I did not have enough time to wonder how they had been caught or who they were before Rei shook his head with a grimace and turned to

Zane. "One of them is the guard who shot Charis and Danica. . . ." He hesitated. "Zane, it's Adelina."

Zane's face whitened; my gut lurched as I considered Adelina's last words to me in a new light. *It doesn't seem appropriate anymore.*

"She wouldn't have hurt my mother," Zane whispered desperately. He pushed past Rei, and then paused before opening the door, bracing himself. "Who is the other?"

"Karl." Now I understood Rei's disgust. He had personally assured me of Karl's loyalty, only to find that the guard had nearly gotten me killed. "Both have confessed. The Royal Flight and palace guard can deal with them, if you wish."

Zane shook his head. "I'll speak to them. Danica?"

I nodded. Unpleasant as it would be, it seemed right that I should face my people—even if only to sentence them.

Rei nodded, and I could tell he agreed with our decisions. He opened the door to the hall for us.

Both assassins' hands were bound behind their backs. Erica was holding Karl's wrists, and Ailbhe held Adelina. The guards' expressions were carefully blank as they detained their own people—and, in Ailbhe's case, his own sister.

"She wasn't supposed to hurt you," Karl instantly protested, before anyone bid him to speak.

"Shut up; they don't care," Adelina responded briskly. She raised her gaze to Zane's, and then looked at me.

Now Karl pleaded with Rei. "I was trying to protect my Tuuli Thea. I knew they couldn't be trusted—"

"You're guilty of treason," Adelina once again interrupted. "No one cares why."

"I care," Zane disagreed. His voice held a wintry chill, which did not quite manage to cover his pain. "I care why you killed my mother, and tried to kill my mate."

"*It wasn't supposed to be poisoned*," Adelina snapped, glaring at Karl. "He gave me the bolt. An avian bolt, so they would be blamed...." Now her gaze turned to me, and it was all I could do not to step back. "The poison was supposed to be weak, just enough to look like someone was trying to harm Charis—without actually doing it."

"And *you* weren't supposed to hit my Tuuli Thea," Karl argued, yelling to be heard over Adelina. "You nearly killed her—"

"I was trying to!" Adelina shouted back. "It was only a mistake I didn't." Her voice softened as she continued. "I saw my Diente, the man I loved, honoring *his* vows no matter how cold and miserable they left him—"

"Would someone just kill her and get it over with?" Karl asked, his calm voice causing Adelina to turn to him.

"I should have skinned you when I first found you in the palace," she retorted. "You were stupid enough to slice open your own Naga. I should have known you were too stupid to—"

"I was stupid to think a snake would keep her word!" Karl answered. "You lied to your own king. Why did I think you wouldn't lie to me?"

"Enough!" Both quieted abruptly at Zane's shout. "Karl, *you* were the one who cut Danica?"

The guard answered bluntly, "Trying to kill you, sir." I had to turn my gaze away, rather than face the young guard's poise.

Zane turned next to Adelina. "You lied to me about Karl."

"Yes . . . sir."

"You tried to kill my mate in the synkal, and in the process killed my mother."

"The poison wasn't supposed to be—"

He held up a hand to silence her. "Yes or no, Adelina?"

She swallowed hard. "Yes. And I'm aware that it's a death sentence. Accident or not, I would impose the sentence upon myself for your mother's death. I only wanted to make sure he"—she nodded at Karl—"was also caught, before he could further defend his Naga by trying to kill you again."

Zane swallowed thickly. "Andreios, can you and Erica see that these two are kept under control until they can be dealt with?"

Rei nodded.

"Good." Zane closed his eyes, drawing a deep breath, and suddenly the vulnerability in his expression was obvious. "Ailbhe, you may be dismissed. You don't need to be involved in this."

I saw the moment of hesitation in every tense line of the white viper's body before he shook his head sharply. "Thank you, sir, but I'll stay. If I can't do my duty now, I have no place in your guard."

Zane nodded gravely. Rei, Erica and Ailbhe escorted the two traitors out.

As soon as they were gone, Zane collapsed against the wall. "I should have known. Gods . . . I trusted her with your life. . . ." He pulled me closer, until I was resting against him. "You could have been killed." He kissed the top of my head.

I lifted my face to meet the kiss, wanting the comfort of his touch as much as I was willing to provide the comfort of mine. The contact was sweet and soft, yet at the same time desperate.

It was Zane who pulled away first. "Danica, I

think . . ." He trailed off and kissed me again, this time briefly, just the barest touch of lips to lips. "I love you."

From a man who frequently uttered eloquent speeches, the tentative declaration was not the most flattering of compliments—especially when every movement he made and look he cast my way had shown the truth long before now.

But coming from the serpent who had once informed me that he did not love me and did not think he ever could, whose cool, polished words could cut to the bone and freeze the Earth's molten blood—whose eyes right now were just a bit dazed, and whose expression was as open and startled as I had ever seen it—the words were more than enough.

"I know," I answered. Then, soft but certain, I answered, "I love you, too."

His smile matched mine and said the same as mine: *I know.*

My prayer is simple, my dear one, my dear one. May you never need understand. My prayer is for peacetime, my child, my child.

Live it well, and this life can be grand.

Also by Amelia Atwater-Rhodes

In the Forests of the Night
"Insightful . . . and imaginative."
—*Publishers Weekly*

Demon in My View
An ALA Quick Pick
"A fast-paced vampire novel with . . . studly [characters] who aren't going to let a little thing like death stand between them."
—*The Bulletin*

Shattered Mirror
An ALA Quick Pick
"An action-packed thriller. . . . Atwater-Rhodes owns a readable prose style and a vivid imagination."
—*Booklist*

Midnight Predator
An ALA Quick Pick
"The plot and characters are so skillfully intertwined that each one moves the story to its thoughtful ending. . . . A must-read."
—*School Library Journal*

Don't miss

Zane Cobriana, cobra shapeshifter, thanks the gods every day for Danica, his hawk pair bond, and the peace their union has brought to the avians and serpiente. Soon Danica will have a child to carry on their royal lines. But what should be a happy time is riddled with doubt.

Syfka, an ancient falcon, has arrived from the island of Ahnmik claiming that one of her people is hidden in the avian and serpiente land. The falcons are more powerful than the avians and serpiente combined, and Syfka shows nothing but contempt for Zane and Danica's alliance. To Zane's horror, his own people seem just as appalled as Syfka is by the thought of a mixed-blood child's becoming heir to the throne. Is Syfka's lost falcon just a ruse to stir up controversy among them? The truth lies somewhere in their tangled pasts—and the search will redefine Zane and Danica's fragile future.

In *Snakecharm*, Amelia Atwater-Rhodes has crafted another suspenseful fantasy set in the complex world of shapeshifters, where faith in one's ideals can be the most powerful force of all.